THE MERRY MISFITS OF MERCER

ASHLEY PERCIVAL

MISADVENTURES MEDIA

All rights reserved.

Copyright © 2025 by Ashley Percival (Misadventures Media) Ontario, Canada

First Edition

ISBN: 9798288011214 (paperback)

No part of this publication may be reproduced in any form, or by any means, electronic or mechanical, including photocopying, recording or any information browsing, storage or retrieval system, without permission in writing from Ashley Percival (Misadventures Media).

The story, all names, characters, and incidents portrayed in this production are fictitious. No identification with actual persons (living or deceased), places, buildings, and products is intended or should be inferred.

Book cover design by: Victoria Davies (vcbookcovers.com)

Editing by: Gary Percival

This book is dedicated to those who spread love in their merry little ways.

PROLOGUE

It was the week before Christmas in Mercer, Ontario. Snow fell softly, enveloping the town in a gentle, white winter glow. Strings of golden lights shimmered above the frost-covered streets, adding a magical touch to the already charming small town.

For Dana Anderson, Reggie Snow, and Wyatt Greene, Mercer wasn't just where they lived. No, Mercer was the place where their stories of love and loss played out publicly. Nothing escaped the notice of this small town's residents, *nothing*.

As Mercer's residents prepared for the holidays, these three merry misfits faced their ghosts of Christmas past, present, and future. They looked to the town's people to help them rediscover love, find laughter amid challenges, and believe in the possibility of happily ever after—if their hearts were willing.

So, grab your hot chocolate and a tissue, or two. Sit back, relax, and enjoy the sleigh ride.

CHAPTER 1

Dana

Like most days, I was startled awake by the incessant beeping of my alarm clock. I hit the button forcefully, not once, twice, but three times before I knocked it onto the floor. I was probably the only person who still used a proper alarm clock besides, maybe, my grandma.

I wasn't sure what had put me into a sour mood, but I was certainly not having it- something was in the air today.

I threw the covers over my head, begging the universe for one more minute under the warmth of my blankets before I was forced awake to face the day. After a quiet minute of contemplation, I growled, threw off the shroud, and padded grumpily across the cool hardwood floor to the kitchen where a fresh pot of coffee awaited me.

Most people knew not to ask too much of me until two cups of dark java pumped through my veins, or else a different type of trouble would brew.

On the kitchen counter, I found my lifeline to society. I tapped the darkened device awake, summoning the technology demon that had taken over my life. I must've left it there last night after going down the rabbit hole of the latest social media hype. As I sipped my black coffee, I wondered if that new purple toothpaste really did work.

I later found out that it doesn't.

The kitchen clock ticked loudly, signalling my daily departure time. I retrieved my beat up thermos from the cupboard and dumped the remainder of the coffee into the stainless steel vessel where I prayed it would stay warm long enough to get to the shop. I needed all the help I could get to stay awake. It was going to be a busy day.

But first, I made my way back to the bathroom where I slathered on my pharmacy brand cosmetics. I took note of the dark bags under my eyes. That was the consequence of staring at my phone until the wee hours of the morning. Other people were 'swiping' and 'liking' on dating apps on their phones, but not me. I didn't have any interest in dating anyone. Ever.

I looked at the clock one last time. Ruby, my geriatric black lab, apparently had no intention of getting up. Who could blame her? The jeans I had so carelessly dropped on the floor last night made a comfortable bed for my furry companion. My bad for not putting my things away, I suppose.

Eventually, after a gentle nudge from my foot, a sleepy sigh emerged from her lips. Ruby waddled across the floor, awaiting her own morning constitutional. I wrenched open the storm door. Frost had formed frozen fireworks on the glass during the night. "You're not going to like this," I muttered to my fur baby.

I held onto the cold handle, my fingers tingling, knowing what came next. Then, holding my breath, I eased the door open and ordered my faithful companion to do her business, but instead of going outside, she looked up at me with her big brown eyes. I felt as if she thought that I was crazy to expect her to go outside.

"Come on, I'm going to be late," I urged. Tardiness was my fault, not hers, but I would never admit that. Eventually, she did what she had to do, often looking back at me with a judgmental expression.

Upon completion, she flew through the front door and buried herself under the blanket in her bed.

The kibble clanged into her metal dish, but she was uninterested. I looked at her as she poked her black nose out from under her blankets. "Suit yourself," I chuckled.

In Northern Ontario, you get used to the frigid temperatures by wearing warm winter gear – in my case, it was a bulky, down-feathered jacket and heavy winter boots. Making my way through freshly fallen snow to my car in the driveway was exhausting, despite the short distance. Then, I had to wrestle with the plug that, if still connected, kept the engine warm enough overnight that it would turn over on command. Luckily, it did, but if I needed help with my car, I knew who to call.

I hopped in, and in answer to my prayers, the engine turned over, albeit reluctantly. I waited while its heater struggled to warm the all-too-cold interior. My morning contemplations exited my mouth in white clouds, disappearing as soon as they were thought. If only I could release my anxieties this way. There had been so much on my mind, making this past year a rollercoaster of emotions; however, in just over a week, the calendar would roll over, and I could finally have a fresh start. New beginnings are always welcome.

The car lurched down the snow-crusted streets. Plows had already been out clearing the roads as best as they could for the morning commuters. I had exactly three sets of traffic lights before I arrived at work. I was one of the lucky ones. Some townsfolk had a much longer commute, so I was grateful for small mercies.

Anyone planning to visit our small village of Mercer, Ontario, dare not blink because otherwise they would miss it- it really is a small place. The main drag is set off from the main highway that connects us to the larger, more civilized cities, if you could call them that. Mercer had exactly one: pharmacy, hardware store, grocery store, post office, coffee shop, bank and pub. We did, however, have two gas stations, two convenience stores, three auto-body shops and twelve churches. Apparently, Mercer was a refuge for sinners.

Given the -25 degree Celsius weather my rust bucket of a car was giving me grief for coming to work today in the cold. It coughed and sputtered as if taking its last breath, but eventually I made it all the way down Main Street and parked my car behind the store. It was good business to leave a parking space out front for potential customers.

Unfortunately, as I was about to open the shop door, I fumbled and dropped my keys into the snowdrift that had accumulated at my feet. Don't worry, I'll spare you the expletive or two that escaped my lips as I tried to retrieve them. Like I said already, there were a lot of sinners in Mercer, and I was no exception.

CHAPTER 2
Reggie

"Damn it!" I cursed as I fastened the last load of logs onto the back of the truck. Somehow, my work jacket got caught in the metal flatbed frame and tore a big hole in the material. I smoothed down the edges of the torn fabric, like that would do anything to fix the damage. A ripped jacket was just something else to add to my recent list of misfortune.

When were things going to start turning around for me? I felt bloody cursed!

In some ways, I thanked my lucky stars. This was the last shipment before Mercer's lumber yard shut down over Christmas. This time of year the business closed for the holiday so that folks could have more time with their loved ones. Well, at least some of us would have more time. Part of me wished the yard would stay open so I could distract myself. Home used to be an oasis, but now it was full of ghosts that haunted me. I shook my head, trying to focus on the task at hand.

"Everything good?" Juan called out from the truck's cab. His cheeks were pink as the cold air nipped at his face. I bet this good looking kid didn't have a care in the world. He would never know what it was like to be me.

I forced a tight smile, nodded and patted the cab door to signal Juan that he was good to go. "Do you have any plans for Christmas, my friend?" asked Juan, as his dimples spread into a gigantic smile. Recently, I had an aversion to happy people like him, especially handsome ones. I used to be that handsome once, or so I've been told.

Beneath my veneer of civility, I wondered why people had to be so damn intrusive. Can't a man work peacefully without someone nosing into his personal life? Betty, my wife, was constantly nagging me about social pleasantries. But, for a man like me, those graces don't come easily.

"The usual family time," I mustered, "nothing special." I looked up at the snowflakes that were falling around me. Trying to think of something polite to say I enquired, "How about you?"

Juan studied me for a moment. Perhaps he was on to my lie. "After I drop off this shipment, I'm headed to the city to see my sister and Abuela." The smile on his face couldn't get any bigger, but as he looked at me, it faded slightly. Perhaps he didn't want an old fool like me to feel bad. No doubt my sour demeanor gave the impression that I didn't think much of the upcoming holiday.

I nodded, hoping the conversation would soon end and I could get back to work. "That sounds," I paused as I cleared my throat and tried not to say anything too inappropriate, "very nice." I looked around, eyeing what other tasks had to be done before the workday was over. I was desperate to get out of this conversation.

"It's very nice. I miss my family a lot." Juan held a gloved hand over his heart. If I didn't know any better, I think I saw a tear drop roll down his face.

I let out a heavy sigh. "I can relate." I scratched my stubbled face with the back of my rough work glove.

After an awkward silence, I nodded and broke the ice, "Well, I'd better get back to it. Don't want the boss yelling at me." I nervously chuckled to myself. I felt the heat rising from my neck, threatening to spread across my cheeks.

Juan stared at me. The smile dropped from his face and he became more serious. "Are you okay, my friend?" Was it really that obvious what was going on? I had done my best to conceal my issues, but maybe I wasn't as clever as I thought.

Where did that come from? What did he know? "Uh, yes." I tried to pretend innocence. "Why do you ask?" I enquired suspiciously. The last thing that I needed was for people to be gossiping about me; there was enough of that in Mercer already. Everyone seemed to know everyone else's business … one of the few things I hated about living in a small town.

Juan looked startled as he removed his gloves. "No reason in particular," he said raising his hands in defence. "I was just concerned about you," he shrugged. "You look like you've been losing weight, that's all." His facial expression appeared to be genuine. Maybe he was legitimately worried about me. I had a bad habit of jumping to conclusions.

I felt my body relax. Juan obviously didn't know anything. "Oh. I've been cutting back on the big meals," which was partially true. I couldn't cook worth a damn, so I was eating less. Truthfully, Betty was the chef in our household. She once told me that I burned water, so, if we wanted to survive, she would do the cooking for us.

"I worry about you. You work hard." Juan's eyes shone with sincerity. "You need to take care of yourself."

I scratched the five o'clock stubble that had begun to sprout from my chin. I had been neglecting myself lately and I supposed it showed.

I wasn't used to people caring about me, not lately anyway. I couldn't help but feel as if I had been abandoned.

Juan wasn't wrong. I needed to figure out how to take care of myself now that I was on my own. I desperately wished that was not the case, but sometimes life hands you lemons.

"I'll bring some tamales on my way back, okay? We'll have a feast and talk about the holidays," Juan offered, trying his best to turn the conversation around so that I could back out of it gracefully.

That food sounded good, but the useless chitchat not so much. I could hear Betty whispering in my ear, *"Be nice, Reginald. Don't be a grumpy old fart."* Suddenly, my shoulders felt heavy from the burden of my mistakes. "Sounds good, Juan. I'll look forward to that." I was still working on changing my tune, but it wasn't easy.

Juan extended his hand down from the truck, and my hand reluctantly met his. He gave me a firm, warm squeeze. It was the most human touch I've had in months to the extent that I was hesitant to let him go, but eventually I did. I had to get accustomed to being alone.

With a roar of the truck engine, Juan started to lurch down the winding dirt road out of the lumber yard. He rolled his window down and stuck his head out. "Feliz Navidad, my friend! See you in the New Year!" he called out, his voice becoming smaller as his vehicle faded out of view. I waved and, when I knew he was gone, I muttered to myself, true to character, "Merry Christmas, my ass."

As I headed inside to get out of the cold, I felt my phone vibrating in my pocket. I put the tip of my work glove between my teeth and tore it off, retrieved the phone and tapped repeatedly on the rectangular screen trying to make the damn thing wake up. When the screen finally illuminated there was a text message from my pride and joy.

Maggie: "Hey, Dad. How're you holding up?"

I sighed, "Not so good, honey."

CHAPTER 3
Wyatt

I enjoyed being alone.

Let me clarify that: I enjoyed being alone while at work. One of my favourite times of the day was around 6 a.m. I liked to come in when no one else was there. I would put on a pot of coffee, inhale the aroma of freshly brewed beans and search for my favourite tunes on my playlist. I would be alone, in heaven, until everyone else rolled in two hours later, much to my displeasure. In the meantime, as soon as the coffee was ready, I'd go into my dad's office and put my feet up onto his desk. He hated that when he was here, that's why I did it when he wasn't around. That man had too many rules, especially for his adult son, a.k.a. *me*. I imagined what it might be like, one day, *if* I took over for my dad.

When I was alone, people, namely my dad, weren't barking orders at me. He was never shy about correcting me if I wasn't doing something right. I guess that's how you learn, but I never thought that I was doing anything wrong in the first place. If it wasn't him on my case, it was angry customers who thought that we were taking too long in the shop. There were other places in town where they could take their cars, if they were that unhappy with the service here. But, whenever an irate customer would ask to speak to the manager, I'd stroll into the office and defer to my dad. Clearly, I wasn't ready to take over yet. He knew how to sweet-talk the customers and assure them that *Lou's Auto Body Shop* was his business, his pride and joy, and that he'd make everything right. They would never know that in his eyes they were wrong. Not only did I not have his gift as he called it, but also it definitely wouldn't be my style, if I were the boss.

I hated having people criticize me or tell me what to do. When you're alone, no one does that or interferes with your life, *ever*. You wouldn't believe the number of people I ran into regularly who asked what I planned to do with my life, if I was thinking of taking over the shop when my dad retired, or worse, when I was going to ask Sabrina Morrison, my girlfriend, to marry me. Don't people have better things to do than to nose around in other people's business? I wish I could tell some people to get a life and get off my back!

There's real trouble when people corner you and try to draw you into unwanted conversation. My life is nobody's business, but the busybodies of Mercer sure did think it was. If ever I answered a prying question, I would try to be as vague as possible. Sometimes I'd be at the bank, or *Lucky's Pub*, and I'd overhear someone saying that Sabrina and I had eloped, broken up, or were having a baby. Gossips never seemed to have their facts straight!

I genuinely believed that I was better off alone. That way, no one would get hurt. But deep down, even if I couldn't or wouldn't admit it, I knew that I couldn't live without my sweetheart, Sabrina. She was my everything.

If I were being honest, I dreamed about living off the grid. Living in a small town in Northern Ontario, you're almost off the grid anyway! I almost had Sabrina convinced that this was the perfect lifestyle. I painted a beautiful picture for her: I would get a few friends to help build a cabin in a yellow wood near a secluded lake, so that she could paddleboard on the crystal clear water. I'd make a small garden so that we'd have fresh produce. We could go hiking, fishing and sit by a roaring campfire every night, holding hands and drinking wine. We'd be far away from everyone who nagged us, judged us, and put pressure on us. It would be perfect. Sabrina was almost in agreement when she burst my bubble. She said that we'd need money to live off and I had to admit that she was right. So much for that pipedream. However, I still held onto the fantasy of living a stress-free life. Maybe one day it would become a reality, but not today. That's for certain.

What were the perks, if any, of being alone? I was trying to figure out if it was my choice or my destiny. Do I choose a life with Sabrina? Or a life alone? This was one of the most difficult things I've had to contemplate in adulthood, and lately, the path I would take consumed my every thought ... which one would it be? It was the choice that would make all the difference.

CHAPTER 4

Dana

When the lock reluctantly opened, I thrust my hip against the wooden door that always seemed to be stuck to get into my shop. That door was no different than everything else in my life that always seemed to need fixing.

The shop was dark, still asleep as it waited for the day to begin. Clumsily, I made my way through the maze of flower shop paraphernalia to the front door where I flipped over the OPEN sign and unlocked the door. The walk-in fridge hummed constantly, protecting its precious contents whose many fragrances would permeate the shop once it was opened so that I could begin to fill the day's orders. I flicked on the lights and all was good, or so I thought.

Last year, following the regretful incident, I decided to open my flower shop, *The Shrinking Violet*. Its name certainly does not reflect who I am. As a matter of fact, I chose the name because it is exactly what I didn't want to become, or how I wanted to be perceived. However, some town folk made fun of me when I opened the store, thinking I was setting myself up to be someone who preferred to live in the shadow of a man, especially after what had happened to me not so long ago. Nothing could be further from the truth. Nervously, I played with the small silver rose that hung on a chain around my neck. I once promised someone special that I'd always be true to myself, and that was a promise I was determined to keep.

And, I did persist with this promise. I still had a few more haters to win over, but my store was a success, and soon I'd be able to finish paying off my bank loan. I was proud of what I had made for myself, even if it came at the cost of a broken heart or two.

At my workstation, I turned on the power bars that illuminated the festive lights, and I marvelled at the holiday cheer surrounding me in my shop. In addition to the usual flower arrangements, a miniature train carrying tiny passengers chugged around a display table and brought to life a winter village. I'd done my best to recreate the magic of Mercer in this holiday display. I had added children tossing snowballs while carolers sang around a miniature twinkling Christmas tree. I even included an ice rink with skating couples. It was just then that the dark side of my character decided to breakup one of those happy couples to add a little realism to the display. Such an innocent act could easily put a damper on the Christmas spirit, so I refrained from destroying their bliss and moved on towards the register. I smiled at the overstuffed teddy bears who wore their finest plaid bows while they eagerly awaited the cuddly arms of a child. Then, after running my finger over a furry ear, I decided to tuck one under the counter for Ruby's stocking.

Recently, I've been having mixed feelings about the holidays. I contemplated spending this holiday alone, unless you counted Ruby. My parents were visiting my aunt in Toronto. I declined the invitation to join them, afraid that my mood would dampen the festivities. After all, over the past year, I had made many life changes, not all of which may have been working for me. Being an independent woman could have its downfalls, but I couldn't dwell on that.

Instead, I found the order requests for the day and busily got to work while the latest holiday country song played low in the background. I must've been lost in thought because I didn't hear Sabrina, my best friend, barge in with a cardboard tray of lattes and a stack of mail.

"Here you go, love," she said. When her hand banged on the hard counter surface, her fingers inadvertently released the paper contents it was holding, and they scattered amongst the white daisy arrangement I was piecing together. "What's on the agenda for today?" Sabrina asked without skipping a beat.

"Thanks for the bevy." I stopped to take a sip; my energy was low this morning. "I'm working on an anniversary arrangement for Mr. Patterson, 30 years married." I smiled weakly. I wondered when it would be my turn to wed, realizing that I was unlikely to date, let alone get engaged and married, after what happened last year.

Sabrina looked down at the arrangement, and said without filter, "I love daisies as much as the next person, but the cheap bastard could've sprung for roses. Am I right?" With calloused fingers she retrieved one of the flowers from his arrangement and, plucking its petals, recited, "He loves me, he loves me not." This melancholy reference was not to my customer, but to her longtime boyfriend, Wyatt.

"Wyatt loves you. Don't be silly." He had actually been my best friend since grade school, but he had been with Sabrina for the last ten years with no proposal in sight. I don't know what was wrong with that man.

I don't even know what's wrong with *me* sometimes.

"I think that Wyatt loves working on cars at his dad's shop and drinking with the guys after work," Sabrina offered weakly.

In my own mind, I knew that he was allergic to commitment ... it was hard not to be when your mom up and left your family without explanation when you were just a kid. Sinners, remember?

"He'll get his act together soon enough." I placed flowers in the arrangement. "Just you wait and see. Men's brains develop more slowly," I said. We both stifled giggles.

Sabrina adjusted her heavy mailbag and said, "I should get going. Message me after work. We can finish our jigsaw puzzle like two old maids." I rolled my eyes at her as the doorbell signalled her exit.

Sabrina and I had resorted to puzzles this last year. I didn't want to be seen in public. I didn't want to be made fun of or hit on. I simply wanted to be left alone to figure out my life. It hadn't been until recently that I'd accepted her invitation to join her and Wyatt for a trivia night at *Lucky's Pub*. I was still somewhat stuck in hibernation mode, and I needed to start living my life in public again.

With my last order of the day completed and placed into the fridge, I cleared my workstation and started to rifle through the mail Sabrina had left me. Bills, tossed. Adverts for pyramid scheme cosmetics, tossed. An order request, set in the 'to-do' pile. And, finally, a red envelope with no return address – my interest piqued.

I inspected the envelope with the eye of a detective. It felt too flimsy to be a holiday card. I took out my silver letter opener and sliced my way inside like a skilled surgeon. A single piece of writing paper slid out into the palm of my hand.

I took a minute to ponder who this could be from.

Who writes letters these days?

I carefully unfolded the paper, smoothing out the creases. I read it not once, twice, but three times.

Dear Dana,

Your shop is a huge success. I knew you could do it. I'm so proud of you. You're the most ambitious person I've ever known. You inspire me.

X

Who was "X"? What kind of letter was this? Where did it come from? I racked my brain, but couldn't think of anyone who would sign their name like that.

Was this a joke?

Most people in town were friendly and approachable. Did people think *I* wasn't friendly or approachable? Did they think they had to write an unsigned letter to me? This made no sense.

I tried not to spiral, but it was too late. If spiralling were an Olympic sport, I'd win a gold medal. I'd probably hold the title of world champion!

Perhaps this was some silly prank? But what would the end game of this prank be? Hopefully, it wasn't that kid, Todd Thompson, who worked at *O'Neil's Groceries* after school. He seemed to have a bit of a crush on me, but the handwriting seemed too mature for a high school kid.

No, I shook my head. It's got to be someone I know. But who?

Suddenly, it dawned on me. Maybe I didn't know who the sender was, but I knew just the person to ask. She knew *all* the town gossip.

CHAPTER 5

Reggie

Once the Mercer Lumber Yard closed for the day and the boss handed out our yearly bonuses, I headed home. Truthfully, I didn't want to go home yet, but I didn't know what else to do. The shops would soon close, and most people would be at home with their families. That was the problem with small towns: there was nowhere to run and hide when you wanted to.

Over time, getting all the stock out of the yard before the end of the year had been running me ragged. For 45 years I had devoted myself to this job and what did I have to show for it? Truth be told, I was avoiding going home. I still couldn't get over the fact that it was less than a week before Christmas, and I was likely going to be alone for the holidays. Well, alone apart from being with Betty's cat, Bruce. I hadn't even bothered to put the holiday lights on the house. I just wasn't in the spirit this year. What was the point of celebrating if I wasn't going to be with the ones I loved?

My ancient truck growled as I maneuvered down the unplowed streets. The noisy engine, coupled with the radio static, drowned out the whiny holiday carols I had no patience for anyway. The holiday didn't bring me any joy this year, only misery.

The night sky shrouded Mercer as I pulled into my driveway. Usually, I'd be coming home to a hot meal made by my wife, but I'd have to get my own meal tonight, again.

Sheepishly, I took a brief glance at the festively decorated houses and the happy families who could be seen through the frosted windows. I couldn't help but be envious. The saying 'Happy wife, happy life' fleetingly entered my mind; all that I could think of was that those poor bastards won't even see it coming if their wives weren't happy. "You're better off alone," I chattered somewhat unconvincingly to myself.

And then there was Bob Collins, my nuisance neighbour whose tacky decorations cluttering his property. Multicoloured lights twinkled on trees, giant blow-up flamingos wearing Santa hats rocked back and forth in the wild winter wind. There was even a Santa wearing flower print shorts riding a surfboard. What was he thinking?! There was so much crap in his yard that it must've been visible from space. I also wondered what his hydro bill was like. Betty would shoot me if I ever did anything as ridiculous as that! Then again, Betty wasn't around to tell me what to do, now was she?

I sat in the truck for a few extra minutes. "Another night alone," I said out loud to myself as I thumbed the creased edges of my holiday bonus. "Why did she do that to me?" I shook my head in disbelief. How much longer would I be punished? I cut the engine and made my way inside the darkened house.

Why was *I* the one who had to change? I mused. There was nothing wrong with me. I placed my keys by the door, boots on the plastic vent warmer, and jacket by the fireplace. I bent down to put logs in the fireplace only to realize that there weren't any. I was out. "Damn it!" The last thing I wanted to do was to go back outside. Could anything else go wrong?

I forced my aching feet into my still cold, soggy boots and swung the back door open. A blast of frigid air slapped my face. Angrily, I stomped through the virgin snow to collect the firewood. With my arms laden I started the awkward trek back to the house. Out of the corner of my eye I could see my annoying neighbour, Bob, and his wife, Suzanne, standing in front of their big bay window. A dazzling white and gold Christmas tree was illuminated behind them. They were hosting their annual get together where Bob dressed up as Santa and handed out gifts to his grandchildren. The holiday celebration was always earlier at their house since their adult kids preferred to head south to Florida to escape the cold, but Bob and Suzanne never seemed to mind.

The truth was, I was jealous of their nice family, beautiful house and big car. In my case, it was just me, Betty, and our daughter, Maggie. Maggie hadn't yet settled down and every time we talked all she seemed to do was complain that there weren't any romantic prospects. She was convinced that there were "No good men out there," as she put it. Sometimes I think she was referring to men like me, and she'd probably be right to think that I wasn't a great man. Betty sure didn't think so, at least not right now.

I paused for a moment, the weight of the logs growing heavier. I couldn't help but feel like a voyeur as I stood in the darkness, soaking in the holiday warmth of my neighbours. Bob was dressed in his weathered Santa suit. I watched as he handed a gift to his wife. She smiled appreciatively at Bob, wrapped her arms around his neck and kissed him hard. She certainly looked happy. An uncomfortable pain twisted in my stomach, the same one I had been feeling for the last month or so. Feelings had always been such a pain for me. Who needed emotions anyway?

I leaned up against the woodpile, taking one last stolen glance at the picture-perfect life next door. I hung my head and headed inside. Warming my frozen heart, however, would have to wait.

Just as I stepped through the door, the bag I was using to carry the firewood split open spilling its contents. Cuss words flew out of my mouth like a fire breathing dragon. Then, to add insult to injury, a splinter caught under my nail, and I couldn't help but yell, "Oh, holy hell!" Betty was always chastising me for my potty mouth and saying that I was nothing but a big baby. I'll never admit that she was right. More woes to add to my list.

As I bent down to sweep the debris, I noticed a trail leading into the kitchen. "What the hell is this?" I wondered. Then I saw it. That damned cat was on the kitchen counter with his head stuck into an open cabinet and chewing on what could have been my dinner. I swatted at him, narrowly missing his furry orange backside. This damn cat wasn't even mine, and I'd been stuck with the little wretch since Betty's departure. She had *insisted* we get him to rid the house of mice, except there weren't any mice before or after getting the cat. She knew that I didn't like cats and just made up some excuse as to why this despicable creature would be of assistance to us. Bruce and I had a love-hate relationship, the emphasis being on *hate*.

If I was being honest, it pained me to blame the cat. It wasn't Bruce's fault. I hadn't been home much. I was ignoring his mealtimes, and as soon as I came home, I was haunted by Betty's ghost. I was haunted by the fights we had, by the words that should or shouldn't have been said and by my mistakes. Bruce was just acting up because he was hungry and lonely, too. I looked around the house to see where the little bugger had gone. I finally eyed him behind the television stand, a low growl erupting from his ginger belly when he saw me look in his direction. "I'm sorry," I mumbled. I was trying to be a better man, but I guess I wasn't quite there yet.

I pulled a can of tuna out of the cupboard and peeled open the lid. The familiar sound almost enticed Bruce from his hiding spot. If I gave him this treat, maybe he'd forgive me. Consider it a feline olive branch, if you will. But the cat still didn't trust me; he hadn't forgiven me just yet. Betty insisted that he not have 'people' food, but she wasn't here to tell me what to do. I was a grown man, and I would do what I wanted. I'd share my meal with Bruce. Besides, I couldn't bear to eat alone. I couldn't do that to myself. So, while Bruce devoured his tasty tuna treat, I hovered over the kitchen counter, eating the same roast beef that I had reheated for the third time this week as well as the remnants of the bread the cat had mutilated an hour before. One more night of this questionable meat and I risked getting a stomach-ache, or worse.

After a good half hour, the fire I had started earlier finally began to crackle. I stoked it until it escalated into a fearsome roar. Drops of melted snow puddled on the floor where my work jacket hung. I didn't care if it made a mess. I didn't have a lot to care about these days.

I sat back in my plaid recliner and contemplated the dilemma that weighed heavily on my mind. Suddenly, Bruce broke my train of thought by leaping into my lap. Apparently, he had forgiven me after all. "What do you want, you rascal?" I asked, petting Bruce and weaving my fingers through his tiger-printed fur. Feeling a little less alone with his company, I ventured to ask, "What do you think, Bruce? Do you think Betty will come home soon? Or have I screwed up everything for good?"

CHAPTER 6

Wyatt

Remember that feeling of being in love? I sure did. I felt it every time Sabrina walked into a room. She was such an amazing woman, and I was head over heels in love with her.

Sabrina was the love of my life- she always has been and always will be. However, our love journey hasn't been smooth. Like most couples, we've had rocky periods, but somehow, we made it through the good and the bad.

Every day, I was lucky enough to see Sabrina at work and at home. She was Mercer's first and only postal woman. During working hours, she'd bring our mail to the shop, give me a glimpse of her beautiful smile, and then saunter off to her next drop. Nothing got me more revved up than seeing her in her navy blue work pants and rolled-up white shirt. When she removed her sunglasses and post woman's cap, she'd give her head a shake, loosening her curly hair that would cascade to her shoulders, just the way I liked it. She was like a walking, talking, working woman pinup girl, and she was all mine.

Damn, I still couldn't believe my luck that a girl like Sabrina wanted to be with a guy like me. Sometimes I thought she could do better. What kind of future did I have to offer her living in a small town, working for my dad? I couldn't think like that. She wasn't superficial like some *other* women. Those are not the things that matter in affairs of the heart.

At exactly 10 a.m., when the shop doorbell chimed, I knew that my princess had arrived. "Hello, handsome," Sabrina purred as she leaned over me. I rolled out from under the car I had been working on, coming face to face with my golden ray of sunshine.

I lifted towards her for a kiss. "Hello to you, too, beautiful." Our lips touched with feather lightness. "How goes it today?" Sabrina took off her work gloves and laced her fingers between mine. I was relieved that she didn't care about my dirty hands; she just wanted to touch.

"Oh, you know. Same old, same old," she sighed. "I've got to go back to the post office to get the truck. Lots of parcels to deliver." She stroked my calloused fingers between her own silky-soft ones. "It's that time of the year," she added wistfully.

I knew that the hectic holidays burned her out. Longer hours, more running around Mercer and the area. She was a busy woman, but she always found time for the people she loved which I admired about her. She always treated me like a priority, and I tried my best to return the sentiment, though I could try a little harder.

"Will you be home tonight for dinner? I could get us some take-out." I brought her hand down towards me and kissed it.

Sabrina smiled at me, "Sadly, not tonight. I'm going to Dana's place."

"Puzzles?" I asked, as if I didn't know.

"Indeed," she shrugged. "Will you miss me?" She leaned in to kiss me again.

"Gross, get a room," groaned my workmate, Fletcher, putting his finger in his mouth to mimic barfing. "No one needs to see that," he wretched in comedic agony.

Sabrina and I laughed. "Fletcher, just because you're a bitter bachelor doesn't mean the rest of us are!" I hollered at him. His laugh echoed throughout the shop.

"I just meant, not all of us want to see your displays of affection," Fletcher whined. He'd been single for a year after he and his girlfriend, Katrina, had broken up. It was obvious that he had been sampling a bit more than just the new brews on tap at *Lucky's Pub*.

Sabrina, joker that she was, leaned in to kiss me multiple times on the face until Fletcher stood up and walked out of the room.

"That'll teach him," she winked at me.

I reached up and brought her face to mine for a few more soft kisses. I couldn't get enough of the taste of her lip gloss. I wouldn't be able to wait to get some more sugar from my sweet.

"Well, I'm off, darling." She gloved her fingers and gave me a glimpse into her big doe eyes.

"Take care, beautiful." She wrinkled her nose at me and headed out of the shop.

Yes, I was a lucky man, alright. So why was I so reluctant to make Sabrina my wife?

CHAPTER 7

Dana

Bean There, Done That was my go-to coffee shop in Mercer. It was my only choice for coffee and the coffee was fantastic. Marnie was the owner, server, and busboy of the shop. There wasn't a single person in town who didn't pass through those doors at least once a week, if not more often.

"Hey honey, what can I do you for?" Marnie asked as she shovelled freshly baked brownies into the dessert showcase. The rich, chocolatey scent wafted through the air. My shoulders slumped. I didn't have time to think about brownies. I needed answers.

I marched into the café, leaving clumps of snow on the tiled floor. My puffer jacket deflated when I leaned over the counter. "I need your help, Marnie." I begged as I shoved my letter in her face. "Any idea what this is about?" I shook the letter for emphasis, hoping she'd get the hint at how important it was to solve this puzzle.

Marnie eyed me from head to toe and said, "Manners, that's what you need. And a mop to clean up your mess." She tilted her chin, signalling for me to look at the trail I was leaving in my wake. While she might be one to help, she'll put you in your place first.

"I'm sorry." I huffed, "I've been thinking about this for the last few hours. It came in the mail this morning." I tapped my fingers impatiently on the counter. Rich O'Neil who owned *O'Neil's Groceries* sat beside me and looked up from his crossword puzzle. He wrinkled his nose and moved to the next seat. "Sorry," I muttered under my breath. I felt like a complete wreck.

After a long silence, Marnie took the paper from my hand and read the letter. Her gold-ringed fingers grazed the single sheet of white paper as if she were trying to read Morse code. Finally, she said, "I don't know. I haven't heard anyone talking about you for a while now." Marnie kept her eyes down; she seemed as if she didn't want to make me feel any more embarrassed than I was already. Her bit of news felt both good and bad.

I shifted on one of the barstools. "I don't know who could've sent it, or what it means." I took the letter back and again attempted to decode it myself. Part of me thought that I should've passed it to Rich beside me, doing puzzles, to see if he could figure this one out instead.

"Maybe someone has a crush on you," Marnie cooed. My stomach lurched. That was the last thing I wanted. My claim to fame was not just breaking hearts but shattering them.

"But who? Why?" I rested my chin on my palm, trying to think about who would want to date me.

"Well, you're a beautiful 26-year-old who happens to run a successful business, but what do I know?" Marnie returned to clearing plates and pouring coffee for the other customers. "Open your eyes, you're desirable." Some of the men in the coffee shop, most of whom worked construction, blushed and looked away when I tried to glance around to see who might be interested in me. I might as well be Medusa turning men into stone if they'd fall for me. I smoothed my hair to check for snakes.

"I doubt it's a crush. Thanks anyway." I zipped up my jacket and headed for the door. I felt foolish for being excited about being someone's potential love interest.

"Don't forget about the mistletoe for the Christmas Eve Market!" Marnie called out. I waved in acknowledgment of her reminder while I headed back down the street to my ivory tower, away from the watchful eye of any gentleman suitor.

CHAPTER 8

Reggie

For more nights than I'd care to admit, I'd been losing sleep. I was experiencing nightmares. Like rotten characters from classic Christmas literature, I was being visited by ghosts from my past. I had disturbing visions of my bad behaviour, my character flaws, and, most distressingly, I was haunted by the day Betty up and left me.

The more I was left alone with my thoughts, the more I realized, uncomfortably, that I deserved to be abandoned.

I was starting to realize that I was a crusty old man, that I could be rigid, often stuck in my ways. Some might say I was stuck in a rut. For instance, every day after work, Betty and I would have dinner together. Then, I would spend three hours or so in the garage working on my old car from high school convinced that someday it would run again. On Saturday nights, I would head over to *Lucky's Pub* for a couple of beers with my buddies to watch whatever sporting event was on the big screen, and then I would come home to work on my car again. On Sundays, Betty and I enjoyed playing euchre at the legion, and then we would come home, and she would cook a Sunday roast. I hated breaking this routine. What's the point of changing? What else is there to do in a small town? But maybe not everything is about what I want, or so I've been told. Like I said, I can be a rigid man.

When I lay awake at night, I also realize that I never apologize. I don't say "I'm sorry" … ever. What should I be sorry for? If I don't hold the door open for someone at the grocery store, it isn't my fault if they can't get through the doors fast enough. If I tell Betty that Maggie is coming home for dinner Thursday night when actually it's Tuesday night, well, both days start with the letter 't', so why am I to blame? Shouldn't she just be happy that her daughter has come home? Betty's always yammering about how saying you're "sorry" goes a long way, but to where exactly?

I don't pay attention to details, apparently—except when I'm at work. Think of all the occupational hazards that could happen in the lumber yard, if I weren't on my toes. I spend most of my day thinking and making sure everyone is safe. Juan sometimes refers to me as the 'safety police' – I take my job seriously. When I come home, I want to relax. I don't want to think too hard. I want to put my feet up and enjoy my time off.

There may have been a time or two when I've forgotten Betty's birthday, and Maggie's too- opps. I may have misplaced outgoing mail that Betty told me needed to be sent urgently, only for me to forget about it until she asked me the following week. It's not like I wasn't going to drop it off in the mail. I'm a busy man! And how could I be at fault when I didn't get the exact gift Betty wanted? If Betty wanted the new casserole dishes with the blue flowers on them, she should've just told me, and I would've asked Bryan at *Patel's Hardware Store* to put it in the back until payday. Or she could've cut a picture of it out of the catalogue and stuck it on the fridge. Damn it, Betty! I'm not a mind reader! Just tell me what you want, woman!

And what if I do get a little upset sometimes? Betty suggested that I might be depressed. Well, some men have a hard time expressing how they feel and can become irritable. To Betty, it seems as if I've been irritable my entire adult life. Why shouldn't I be? I've been stuck in the same job for 45 years never once moving up in position … not for lack of trying. What's worse is that the older I get, the fewer opportunities are available to me. The younger guys fresh out of school scoop up the well-paid jobs. The boss said it's because they have a college diploma, and I don't. How is that my fault? I'm a hard worker. Truthfully, my body may retire before I do. Maybe I was a little down in the dumps, but my life hasn't been all bad. It just hasn't turned out the way I had hoped it would turn out when I asked for her hand in marriage all those years ago. Sometimes I feel as if I have failed her as a husband.

I tossed and turned most nights, the bed sheets wrapping around me, trapping me. Would I ever break free from these chains of nightly haunting? Or would I be stuck in this torment forever?

CHAPTER 9
WYATT

Finally, peace and quiet. I took off my steel-toed work boots, trudged through the living room, and sank into the old, plaid couch. Tonight, Sabrina was at Dana's house putting puzzles together, something they've been doing for the past year because, well... it didn't matter why. What mattered was that they were currently enjoying each other's company while I was relaxing at home, alone, with my feet up, watching a hockey game.

I took a deep breath, tilted my head back, and enjoyed the silence. That was until my dad got home. "Hey, son! Miss me?" his lame joke fell flat as he slid heaving bags of groceries onto the countertop. "I was thinking, you want salad and wings for dinner?" There was commotion in the kitchen as my dad, Lou, slammed cupboard doors shut.

A small grumble erupted from my throat. Couldn't a guy be alone for a few minutes? My day had been full of commotion at the shop, not to mention the hectic gift shopping.

"What's that, my boy?" he asked as he leaned against the living room doorframe. I didn't understand how my dad could have any energy after such a tiring day at the shop.

I looked up at him from the television and said, "Sure. That sounds good." I smiled at him. I enjoyed spending time with him, but I wished he had a hobby outside of work instead of hanging out with me. For most of my life I sensed that he was lonely. I hoped that would change one day.

Dad patted the doorframe, confirming our menu, and headed back into the kitchen. "Hey, have you heard from your sister?" Dad called out from the kitchen. He continued banging dishes around as he prepared our feast.

I had forgotten about that little brat. "No, have you?" I hollered at him as he began washing the lettuce. "Oh, you know her." The salad spinner whooshed. "Work and partying." More washing and chopping of vegetables could be heard from the kitchen.

"I can never get that girl to respond to me." Dad said, with a playful irritation. Typical Rachel, living in her own little bubble, and soon she'd come home for the holiday and burst mine.

That's the kind of response we got from Rachel these days: none. We had come to expect it from her. She graduated from interior design school last year and had been staging apartments in Toronto for a real estate agent. Finally, with some money of her own in her pocket, she was going wild. Dad and I tried to talk some sense into her about saving for the future. Rachel, the wild child, told us to "live a little and enjoy life," something we couldn't get used to. Wasn't she worried about rainy days?

"If you hear from her, please let me know." Dad sounded worried. It was hard for him when she moved away to the city. I couldn't do that to him; I couldn't leave Mercer. So, I decided to pursue an apprenticeship and take online courses to learn the trade. One day, I was expected to take over my dad's shop; whether I wanted to or not was a different story. I couldn't just up and leave my dad. What would he do if both of his kids left him?

"Yup," I called out, lacking enthusiasm.

Once dinner was ready my dad sat down beside me on the couch. We had our coffee table set with place mats so that we could watch television and eat. Dad's meals were certainly better than those frozen dinners my grandparents used to have on their rickety TV dinner stands. They'd watch game shows, eat and be in bed by 9 p.m. which didn't sound too bad to me. Dad and I were the proverbial odd couple, living the bachelor life together; at least we liked the same food and the same things on television. You'll never get those years back, spending time with your dad.

The thing was, we weren't really living the bachelor life because we frequently had a third wheel…Sabrina. Even though she had her own place, a basement apartment at Marnie's sister's house, she often spent time with dad and me, complaining that her place was too cold and damp. She much preferred the crackle of our fireplace. Truthfully, I think she liked to hog my king-size bed. I had to cling to the corner every night. I didn't know how such a small woman could take up so much space – not just in my heart, but also in my bed.

If I were being honest, I think Sabrina slept at my house almost every night, mostly going home just to wash her clothes. That was alright with me. Even though I enjoyed my alone time, I much preferred the company of the woman I loved.

It was 10 p.m., and the game was nearly over. Dad had fallen asleep on the couch, while I was glued to the television, eager to see who would score the final goal. Just as my team made an epic slap shot, I heard the jingle of keys in the lock. I assumed that Sabrina was coming home, but I was quite wrong.

"Hi, honeys! I'm home!" My little sister's voice squeaked throughout the house like an unwanted mouse. "Where is everybody?" Rachel rolled in her designer luggage, the wheels grating against the hardwood floor. I don't know how she could afford all that stuff. Dad had helped pay for school, but she seemed to have more than enough money to spend on ... stuff, so much stuff!

"Oh, there you are," my sister sneered at me. Her sweet voice turned menacing. It's true that sibling rivalry never dies. "Are you just going to sit there, or are you going to help me?" She could be a demanding little thing, a true princess.

"I thought you were one of those 'independent women?'" I mocked. She was always posting things on social media about not needing men in her life, but who did she reach out to if she needed her car fixed, or a little extra rent money? *Me*. Big brother, that's who.

"Hardy Har, *idiot*." She playfully shoved my shoulder and then wrapped her arms around me. Her annoying perfume stung my nose. Did she dump the whole bottle on herself? How could she stand to wear that stuff? People must collapse dead in her wake.

When she pulled away from me, I craned my neck for a breath of fresh air. I think her stench startled dad awake; his eyes nearly bulged out of his head. In our defence, he and I were used to scented deodorant and car oil, not whatever witch's potion my sister wore.

"Dad! Wyatt's being mean to me!" Rachel tattled in her high-pitched voice.

"Grow up," I hissed at her. I was ready to knock that princess off her pedestal.

"No, *you* grow up," she challenged me.

"Children! Enough!" Our dad bellowed.

See what I mean?

After a few tense moments, we reconvened. "Anyways, where's darling Sabrina?" Rachel peered into the bedrooms as if she thought she was hiding from her. "I've missed her."

"She's at Dana's place. She might be back in a bit." No sooner had the words come out of my mouth than my beautiful girlfriend stepped inside the house.

"Rachel!" Sabrina wrapped her frigid arms around my bony sister and squeezed her tight. "I didn't know you were coming home for Christmas!" One of the many things I loved about Sabrina was how much she loved my family. From the moment she met them she bonded instantly with everyone. She wasn't just my girlfriend - she was family.

"Girl," Rachel's annoying new catch phrase, "it's been a minute, hasn't it?" Who possessed my sister? Why was she talking like that? Sabrina laughed along with her. "What's new?" Rachel cooed as she took Sabrina's hands, inspecting them. "No ring?" Rachel gave me the side eye, and Sabrina recoiled her hands in embarrassment. "Wyatt, what's wrong with you?" she scolded me. Another person who couldn't mind their own business.

When will people leave me alone about a proposal? I'll get to it when I'm good and ready!

"Don't you have something to do?" I said, crossing my arms and urging her to leave well enough alone. I needed to go to the hardware store to get a human-sized mousetrap.

"Don't be silly! I'm here to spend time with my daddy, big brother and sister-in-law," Rachel linked her arms through Sabrina's. For a moment, I thought I saw Sabrina glance at Rachel, as if to say, "I know", but maybe I was seeing things – after all, it had been a long day, and it was getting longer by the minute.

Ever since I could remember, every holiday card and every piece of mail Rachel sent me was always addressed to Mr. & Mrs. Greene. However, Sabrina and I were *not* married. Even though we had talked about it and around it, we had never taken the leap. Not yet anyway.

Moving on, I questioned Rachel about where she planned to sleep, but dad scolded me and offered her his room.

"I'll take the couch," he said. Everyone always accommodated the princess.

"Are you sure, Daddy?" Rachel said, obviously feigning sincerity, her voice thick with sugar.

"Anything for my baby girl," was dad's reply. As soon as his back was turned, Rachel stuck her tongue out at me. Siblings can be *so* annoying. I had no choice but to retaliate.

So much for peace and quiet. It looked as if I'd be trapped in a full house for the holidays, whether I liked it or not.

CHAPTER 10

Dana

The Christmas Eve Market was a cherished Mercer tradition. Each year vendors hosted a market at the legion, providing last-minute holiday ideas for procrastinating shoppers. Typically, shopping online was slow, or the highways were too treacherous to reach the big city stores. So, this market over the years became a much appreciated festive shopping hub for residents, and a big boost for local businesses.

As I walked back to my store to finish a birthday arrangement, Bryan was in front of the legion, comically trying to untangle a string of multicoloured lights.

I looked behind poor, awkward Bryan and took a minute to soak in the setup for the market. Outside the legion, there was a courtyard made mostly of cedar shrubs and an arched birch walkway where white lights glistened in the snow. I saw the hook where my mistletoe would be placed on the night the market opened. It was the perfect photo-op for lovers to have a Christmas kiss. I smiled, thinking about how great the market would be. I shifted my gaze to watch Bryan as he embarrassingly tried to untangle the string of lights, not unlike trying to solve a Rubik's cube. He only seemed to make the mess worse. I couldn't help but shake my head at the poor shmuck.

His moment of frustration quickly dissipated when he looked up to see me watching him. "Afternoon, Dana!" he called out, his smile stretching from ear to ear. Because I wasn't in the mood for happy people, much preferring solitude and bitterness these days, I tried to sneak into my shop. I knew just how relentless he could be, and I wasn't in the mood for conversation.

"Oh hey, Bryan." I pressed my hands against my scarf as I tried to decide what little white lie that I needed to tell to extract myself from this awkward situation. I might as well have been the shmuck stuck with the Christmas light dilemma, caught in a festive spider's web so to speak.

Bryan dropped what he was doing and trekked through the snow toward me. The swish of his snow pants grew louder the closer he came. Instantly, I knew I was in for a long one. Once he reached me, Bryan started talking about business at the hardware store and the number of power tools ordered as presents for the holidays. As usual he droned on, endlessly. Like the indiscreet elf he was, Bryan shared who was getting what as gifts. For some reason, he thought I'd care. I tried my best to smile and nod, but all I could think about was the letter. I needed to solve that mystery, fast.

"So, are you coming to the market?" he asked, looking back at the tangled mess of bulbs and wires.

"Um, yeah. I'm making the mistletoe." I glanced at my storefront and considered whether or not I could make a break for it. I ultimately decided against it. If I fell and broke my leg, I doubt that Ruby would pull me on a sleigh for our walks.

"Hoping someone will give you a Christmas kiss?" he jested. At that, I blocked him out and tried instead to focus on a mental list of secret admirer suspects to cross off my list.

"Perhaps," I said, half listening. In the error of my ways, Bryan took my comment as some sort of invitation.

"Cool, maybe I could take you out for a drink tonight. We could practise..." He didn't get a chance to finish that sentence before I cut him off.

"You know, I think I'm busy tonight." It would be rude to tell him that I would be busy for the rest of my life, but I couldn't say that now, could I? "Maybe another time." I began to make my way back to my shop. I had invested enough time in Bryan, and I would need a plan to avoid him for the next week.

"If you change your mind, let me know!" Bryan called after me. Maybe he thought that because I took the time to listen to him, it was an invitation for romance. Sorry, Bryan, but no thanks. With him, there'd be too much talking and not enough action, if you catch my drift.

I slammed the shop door shut, and the bell rang in my ears. The warmth of the heater felt like a light sting on my cheeks, as if the store was scolding me for being such an idiot. These days, I deserved a metaphorical slap in the face.

I had to shake off this letter business. It was just a nice letter, nothing more. No one would want to have anything to do with me. I had purposefully shut myself off from society, well, Mercer society, and I was doing my own thing.

"Get over it, Dana. Move on," I tried to tell myself. With no one else in the shop, I could give myself a pep talk, couldn't I? Obsessing over a silly letter was the last thing I needed right now. A vibration in my pocket brought me back to reality. I pulled out my silver phone.

Thankfully it was a diversion - an alert for three new orders to process before Christmas Day. I had better get to work.

For the rest of the day, I tried to get my secret admirer out of my head. Marnie didn't know who it was, and her shop was the busiest spot in town where gossip flowed just as much as her coffee did. I couldn't stop thinking about it. This secret letter was consuming me.

I paused after closing the register at the end of the day. The best detective in town was none other than our local mail carrier. She knew all the town folk and heard all the town gossip, and, fortunately, I had a direct connection with her. It was time to commiserate with Sabrina.

CHAPTER 11

Reggie

Sometimes I was trapped in those nightmares all night long. I swore I could feel the cold sweat drip down my temples. There were nights I rustled so much that old Bruce didn't even want to sleep at my feet. I couldn't blame him.

The nightmare that haunts me the most was the day that Betty left me.

All these faults of mine, and probably a few more, became too much for Betty to handle. The last straw occurred when I balked at her Sunday supper. I should've just kept my damn mouth shut! Why couldn't I have just left well enough alone?

That particular evening was vividly etched in my mind. I relive it almost every night.

As I stirred in my red flannel sheets, I pictured Betty making her grandma's Shepherd's Pie recipe in the kitchen. We had bought a new oven when the one that came with the house had finally kicked the bucket. Betty was having trouble with the oven controls and hadn't quite mastered the new appliance yet. I had just come into the house after working on my car. I had a kink in my hand from tightening the bolts on the wheels. Betty had been nattering on to me about who knows what when I walked past her to grab a beer from the fridge. I plunked down in my recliner and yanked the lever, springing the footrest to life. She continued, raising her voice to me as I turned on the television to find a football game to drown her out.

"Well, what do you think of that idea?" Betty asked, annoyed. I didn't respond because I didn't know what the hell she was going on about. I turned up the volume some more; I couldn't quite make out what the sportscaster was saying over the sound of Betty clanging the dishes in the kitchen and nagging me.

Again, she said, "Reggie, I asked you a question." She marched over to me, snatched the remote from my hand, muted the television, and shot me a glare that pierced not only my eyes but also my heart.

Didn't Betty know that I had had a hard week? Didn't she know that I'd injured my back lugging materials around the lumber yard?

Happy wife, happy life… consider this a warning if you ever think about getting married.

I summoned the courage to speak to her, sensing that she was about to rip my head off. "Yes, dear. That sounds good." I smiled, trying to look past her at the score.

Betty stared at me, narrowing her eyes. "What sounds good?" She folded her arms across her chest, testing me.

"I'll do whatever you'd like to do." I smiled and sheepishly tried to make eye contact with her. I could see the flames of frustration burning brightly in her eyes.

A small, hesitant smile spread across her face. "Really? Reggie, I thought you'd never agree to this!" She leaned down and wrapped her arms around me. Her wool sweater grazed my cheek. What did I just agree to? I felt panic surge through my veins.

I pondered for a moment, trying to think about how I could recover from this situation and understand what she was talking about. "So, tell me more about this plan of yours."

Good save, Reggie.

"Martha down at *Holiday Travel* said that there was a two-for-one package deal to Hawaii, and I thought it was about time we made plans to go. You know how I've always wanted to go to Hawaii, Reggie." My bride beamed as she began to share more about this supposed trip we were going on.

As she continued to drift further into delusion, I nearly choked on my beer. "Hawaii!" I tried to casually laugh to cover up my surprise. "Betty, that sounds *expensive*." I felt as if I was going to hyperventilate. I was dizzy thinking about the dollar signs associated with this plan of hers.

"At first, I thought so, too." Betty made her way back to the kitchen counter. "But Martha gave me this breakdown." She hurried over to the counter and grabbed the brochures. When she returned, she practically tossed them into my lap. "Here, take a look." She flipped through the colourful pages and energetically pointed to a volcano tour, a hula class, and "Take a look at this, deep sea fishing! I thought you'd enjoy that."

I tried my best to look interested, nodding along as she talked about this adventure of hers. When she finally flipped to the back of the travel package, the price tag, in bold font, practically slapped me in the face. "Betty," I slowly cautioned myself before proceeding, "I'm not sure we can afford this." I couldn't believe that she was asking for a trip right after we had just bought a new oven!

Betty's smile faded. "Why not? Your holiday bonus will more than cover it." I hated it when she frowned; the last thing I wanted was to disappoint her.

"We just got the new stove," I gently reminded her. I shook my head, trying to signal to her that this trip wasn't a good idea now.

"Yes, so?" she looked at me quizzically.

"That was a gift," I gulped, "for you." I could feel beads of sweat forming around my hairline, but I didn't think that there was enough sweat to extinguish the fire on my cheeks.

Betty let out a laugh, "A stove is a necessity." She stood up and returned to tend to her pie. "A stove is hardly a gift for a wife. It also serves *you*."

I could feel myself becoming annoyed. Betty was acting like a child. "And then we had the large vet bill for Bruce," I said.

"Bruce is family," Betty inhaled sharply, appalled by my comment.

"Bruce is your cat, not mine," I huffed.

"He choked on the nuts you were eating and left out." As if Betty was going to blame *me* for the dumb cat.

"Are you saying the stupid cat choking on an almond was my fault?" My voice bubbled with anger. I wasn't going to back down from a fight, especially not a fair one.

Betty shrugged as if to silently agree that it was indeed my fault. She'd regret that comment. Just you wait, Betty Snow.

"I'm going to use the rest of the holiday bonus on the car," I told her firmly. I wanted to walk over to the fridge to grab another beer. I usually ask her to fetch me one when I'm watching the game but now didn't seem like the right time to ask her for any favours. Before I could get up, I was frozen in my tracks by my wife's response.

"Excuse me?" she boomed, looming over me. I was so startled that I shook in my recliner. "Big purchases are to be made together, not separately. You can't spend it on the car; I forbid you!" She stood tall with her hands on her hips, holding my gaze, unwilling to back down.

I pushed the footrest of the recliner down and slowly rose to meet her face to face.

"Do I need to remind you that I'm the breadwinner in this family?" We circled each other like two dogs preparing to brawl in the streets. "I'll spend the money as I please."

Betty stepped closer, challenging me. "What did you just say to me?" she whispered angrily.

What did I just say? I never know when to keep my big mouth shut.

"You will not speak to me as if I'm subservient to you." She pressed her finger into my chest.

"I'm sorry, Betty, but the money has been spent. I've already put in an order at *Lou's Auto Body Shop*." I raised my hands up in the air, as if signalling that there was nothing left to do or say.

There was a deafening silence between us, and for the first time in our marriage, I think I felt scared. Happy wife, happy life, they say. I certainly wasn't making choices to keep Betty happy.

"Reginald Douglas Snow, you will call down to that shop and you will cancel that order. Now!"

I stared at her. There was no way I was going to do that. The car was almost ready to run; I was so close to having it finished. Didn't she know how important that car was to me? I had imagined taking her on drives through the countryside, the wind blowing through her head of curls. Now, she was just being stubborn.

"No," I said firmly.

"Reggie, you have no idea what you've done," she whispered through clenched teeth.

The tension was abruptly cut by the sound of the fire alarm blaring in the kitchen. Betty brushed past me, nearly knocking me back into the recliner. Behind us, grey clouds of smoke billowed out of the oven. I rushed over to crack open the windows and the front door while she fanned the flames in the kitchen. I grabbed the fire extinguisher and blasted the oven, spreading white foam everywhere.

Betty reached into the oven and pulled out the charred pie, tears welling in her eyes. "Look what you made me do, Reggie!" Betty cried out. "Dinner is ruined!" She slammed the pie onto the counter, turned, and refused to look at me.

I decided to retreat to my recliner in the living room. What more was there to say? We've had arguments before, and we've always recovered from them.

As I settled into my favourite perch, I mentioned to Betty, "Don't worry. I'm sure there's something else you can whip up for dinner. You always do." I gave her a knowing smile, confident that she could handle this situation without issue. Little did I know that the pie wasn't the only thing about to go up in flames.

Suddenly, my world imploded, and I would be the one to light the match. "Reggie, you don't appreciate me," Betty cried. Her voice trembled as she fought back tears. I hated it when she cried.

I swung the chair around to look at her. "That's not-" I could barely finish my sentence.

"I've been your wife for almost four decades, and you've not once put me first." She hastily tore off her apron and threw it on the kitchen floor. "You're always thinking about yourself!" Betty marched over to the front foyer and grabbed her coat and purse.

"Where are you going?" I assumed she was popping down to the grocery store to get something for dinner. I would have preferred if she had waited until she wasn't upset to drive. I didn't want her getting into a fender bender with one of the neighbours.

The tears ceased; Betty turned to face me. "I'm leaving you." She stood tall, confident in her decision.

"What are you talking about?" She was heading out the door, but she couldn't be serious about leaving me, could she?

"You old fool, I'm done with this marriage. You can find a new wife because you don't respect me!"

Before I could say anything else, she stormed out the front door, got into her rusted old car, and peeled out of the driveway. I got up and walked towards the open door. A cloud of smoke puffed up behind the car as she sped away.

I was dumbfounded. What did she even mean? As I stood at the door, confused, Bruce brought me back to reality. He weaved his way between my ankles. "What do you want?" I grumbled at him. Bruce purred and leapt into the recliner, promptly curling up into a ball on my broken throne. I felt as though he was mocking me, telling me "I told you so".

I can't believe Betty did that. At the time, I thought she was being unreasonable. The truth is, she was right. I didn't consider her. I only thought about myself. I've been a selfish old man.

What had I done? How could I ever get the love of my life back?

CHAPTER 12

WYATT

Like many men, I was terrible at gift giving. The only person I had any gifting sense for was my dad. He was easy – a power tool, a hunting jacket, or World War II books. And Rachel? Forget her! She really didn't need any gifts with her new, fancy job, but I figured I should get her something, or I'll never hear the end of it. And then there was Sabrina's gift. Damn, I was stumped! She liked outdoor things, but this year, I had no idea what to get her for the holiday.

Rachel, my not-so-dear sister, grilled me so much this morning about my relationship with Sabrina that I felt compelled to leave the house on my day off to think about what I should gift my girlfriend. Rachel kept suggesting jewellery, or better yet, an engagement ring, but panic filled my chest.

Why does everyone focus so much on marriage? Shouldn't people figure out who they are first? Sometimes you need to grow separately before you can grow together.

I found the perfect opportunity to leave the house when Rachel had her mouth full of peanut butter toast. Before she could get a word out, I slipped out the door and headed into town. I went to *Patel's*

Hardware Store, where I could do double duty - pick up my dad's gift and ask the guys for assistance with other matters of the heart.

"Morning, Wyatt!" Ramesh Patel, the owner of the hardware store, called out to me. He was hanging ornaments on a wooden pegged display at the front of the store. His face lit up when he saw me and he asked, "What can I do for you today, young man?" I admired how cheerful Ramesh always seemed to be, as if he didn't have a care in the world.

"Here to pick up the wireless drill I ordered." I opened the invoice and handed it to him.

Ramesh studied the page, finding what he needed to retrieve the parcel. "Excellent, I'll be back in a jiffy." His khaki pants swished as he moved swiftly toward the back of the store.

Another familiar voice greeted me, "Hey, man. How's it going?" Bryan reached out to shake my hand. I had always liked Bryan. He's a bit of a talker, sometimes to the point of wishing you were hard of hearing, but he means well.

"Not too much, and you?" My head was overheating so much from the temperature in the store and the thoughts in my head that I removed my toque.

"Same. Did you hear about the new table saws we're getting in? We've got a ton on order. Mr. Collins is getting one this year, and maybe your dad." That got my attention. Who would be gifting my dad a table saw? I doubted that it would be Rachel. She usually chose something impractical like an itchy wool sweater that she thought was stylish.

"My dad?" I asked. "Who got that for him?" No one came to mind who would buy him such an expensive item. This was perplexing.

Bryan pretended to lock his mouth shut as he feigned tossing away an imaginary key. It was too late though. The big mouth had already given himself away. "I can't tell you. Santa is watching," he leaned in and giggled like a little kid.

"Right," I trailed off. Perhaps my dad got it for himself; I know I picked up a few things for myself – why not?

After the awkward moment passed, he asked, "Is Rachel coming home?" Suddenly, I was struck by a brilliant idea.

"Why yes. Are you interested in seeing her?" The wheels in my head were turning. I could get her out of my hair for a few days by pawning Bryan off on her. "I bet she'd love to hear from you." With that seed planted, I jotted down her details on the nearest piece of paper. As a quickly conceived backup plan, I suggested, "If you play your cards right, you just might run into her tonight at *Lucky's Pub*." I winked at him.

OMG! Was I socially pimping out my sister? It certainly wasn't difficult dismissing that moment of guilt.

His eyes widened. "Really? You wouldn't mind if I took your sister out?" Bryan's voice cracked. Perhaps he was on to my wicked plan.

"Not at all," I placed a dishonest hand over my heart. "You're a great guy. She'd be thrilled to go out with you." I could barely contain myself. Rachel had been annoying me ever since she got home; this was payback – I sure hoped she would enjoy all of Bryan's stories.

"Awesome, thanks Wyatt." Bryan looked pumped. "Your sister and I have so much to catch up on!"

"I bet you do," I smirked. "I bet you do."

Just then Ramesh returned with the drill that I had ordered. After signing the receipt, I seized the opportunity to seek the advice I had come to the store for.

"Say, if you guys have a minute, I'd love to ask for your opinion." Bryan and Ramesh looked at each other, bemused. I blurted out, "What should I get Sabrina for Christmas?"

They both stood back, mouths gaping open in shock. "You haven't bought anything yet for your darling girlfriend?" Ramesh asked, horrified.

"Yeah, like, Christmas is only days away," Bryan reminded me, as if I didn't know.

"Well, the shop has been really busy." Instantly, I realized how lame that must have sounded, so I quickly added, "It's not like I haven't been giving it some thought. I just haven't made a final decision."

Bryan and Ramesh exchanged a knowing look, as if to say I was in trouble. "Well, maybe there will be something at the Christmas Eve Market for you to get," Bryan offered. That wasn't a bad idea, but I wanted to get her something before then, just in case I ran out of time.

"I know!" Ramesh perked up, "Why not a pretty, gold necklace?" That seemed rather pricey on my budget.

Just at that moment Reggie Snow barged in demanding service. He mumbled something about a torn bag. Reggie was a nice guy, but he sometimes lacked manners.

When nobody acknowledged him, Reggie asked, "What are you guys talking about?" he snuffled as he adjusted to the warmth of the store.

"Wyatt was looking for inspiration for a Christmas gift for Sabrina," Bryan said.

"Oh, is that all." Reggie grumbled. "And? What ideas did you come up with?" Reggie asked half interested, scratching his chin.

"I suggested a gold necklace," Ramesh replied. Bryan nodded in agreement.

Reggie looked shocked and said, "Once you start buying her jewelry, she'll expect this," he pointed to his ring finger. To be honest, the necklace idea sounded too expensive. Besides, I was saving up for something else I'd been considering giving to her, but I wasn't sure if I had settled on it yet.

"It's just jewelry," Ramesh huffed, "that's not the step before a wedding ring." Ramesh tried to assuage Reggie's concerns, but he should've tried to calm me because my heart was racing so fast that I thought it was going to burst out of my chest!

"You could ask her to marry you on Christmas Eve," Bryan suggested. "That would be a gift to remember." Seeing the panicked look on my face, he added, "But, only if you wanted to."

I tried to force a smile. More people were trying to pressure me into marriage, but I just wasn't ready to go down that road, yet.

For a moment, I thought Reggie was coming to my rescue. Instead, he grunted and said, "Wives are expensive, and divorces are more expensive." I cocked my head and raised my eyebrows, uncertain of what he was implying.

A moment of deafening silence was broken by Reggie who suggested, "What about a toaster? It's practical, and she probably uses one every day. Or maybe a thermos." I had to admit that I appreciated practical gifts, but this wasn't about me. I don't think Sabrina would appreciate a small appliance at this stage in our relationship- what woman would?

"What are you getting your wife?" Bryan asked Reggie. His jaw dropped. He looked very uncomfortable.

"Oh, I don't know," he groaned. "We don't do that anymore," he said, looking perturbed.

Ramesh gasped. "You aren't getting something special for your wife?" He shook his head feverishly, "I do, or I'd be kicked to the curb!" Ramesh broke out into a fit of giggles. Was the hardware store full of childish men? The rest of us uncomfortably joined in.

While the men were in an awkward fit of laughter, I glanced at Reggie. The smile on his face had faded. Maybe finances were tight at home. I knew he'd come into the shop earlier this week to cancel a special order for a custom leather steering wheel.

"Christmas is about spending time together, isn't it? Not just about gifts?" I added, trying to protect Reggie's honour.

The men cleared their throats and nodded, "You are exactly right, young man. Sorry, Reggie," Ramesh offered. Bryan voiced the same sentiment.

"Well, I'm off. Places to go, things to do, people to see, as they say." And, at that, Reggie seized the opportunity to turn and rush out of the store. The three of us were left standing there bewildered by his strange behaviour. I sure hoped Reggie was okay.

CHAPTER 13

Dana

"Well, well, well." Sabrina entered my house with the gusto of a sitcom neighbour. "Look what the cat dragged in." She took off her satchel and dropped it on the floor with a dull thud. She's my best friend, but her entrance wasn't the most graceful thing I'd ever seen.

She marched into the living room and plopped herself onto the couch. The stockings on the mantel swung in her wake.

"Let's see it," she insisted. Without hesitation, she snatched the letter from my hands. I watched as she scanned the envelope and then studied the contents with expert attention. With bated breath I waited while she completed her assessment, and, hopefully determined the identity of the sender.

"Well?" My eyes nearly bulged out of my head in anticipation.

"I got nothing," she said, tossing the contents onto the coffee table and narrowly missing her piping hot chai tea.

"What do you mean you 'got nothing'? You're the one who delivered it to me! Surely you figured out something?" I quickly bent down to pick up the evidence. It would be just my luck if liquid were to spill on it, ruining the cryptic message.

Sabrina lifted her cup to her lips. "There's nothing to tell you." She blew on the hot drink. "There's no return address." She took a sip. "The processing stamp is from here." She gulped with satisfaction. "Whoever sent you that letter likely lives in town."

Once again, I racked my brain, trying to think of who might want me. "Why not just take a chance and speak to me directly?" I rubbed my forehead, willing a list of potential suitors to pop into my mind.

Sabrina's signature laugh echoed through the house. "You're a bit fickle," she pointed out. "Understandably," she corrected herself. If anyone else had said that to me, I likely would've slapped them.

"Isn't that the pot calling the kettle black?" I fired back at her.

"Touché," she nodded in my direction. She adjusted her peacock blue wool socks while getting comfortable. "So, who has a crush on Dana and is too shy to say something to her face?"

Always the detective, Sabrina busted out a pen and paper. "Let's start from the top." She listed some of my childhood crushes, whom we immediately ruled out. Then, we moved on to a few guys who lingered a little too long at our pub table a few weeks ago. "Who else could there be?" Sabrina drummed her pen on the tabletop. "Anyone come into the store an unusual number of times?" she wondered.

I paused for a moment, "Not really."

"Which is it, Dana? 'Not really', or 'no'—those are two different things." Sabrina was always so direct, sometimes to the point of being annoying.

"No," I replied. But at that precise moment it occurred to me that someone had made an unusual move today, "Bryan," I blurted out.

Sabrina spat her tea back into her cup. "Really?"

"I know," I rolled my eyes. Could it be possible that Bryan, of all people, had a crush on me? Was he the mystery man behind the letter?

Sabrina sat quietly for a minute. "He's kind of cute," she purred.

"Being dull does not make up for being 'kind of cute' in my book," I replied. Immediately, I regretted coming off with such an insensitive comment, but Bryan simply wasn't my type.

My best friend stared at me blankly. I couldn't comprehend where her mind was going. Then, she whispered, "Not my type either. I'd rather die alone in a cabin than listen to one more of his boring stories." She shuddered at the possibility of either of us being in a relationship with him.

"Then why would you pawn me off onto him?" I shoved her onto the couch.

"I don't want you to die alone!" Sabrina laughed, shielding herself with a pillow.

I reached over to the coffee table and grabbed a handful of candy canes. "And what, you're willing to die alone rather than be with him?" I tossed a candy cane at her, but she shielded herself with her pillow.

Sabrina raised her hands in surrender. "You're right, I was just teasing you. Relax." She leaned over and picked up where we had left off with the puzzle. "I might not know the answer to your dating dilemma, but I'm damn good at finishing these puzzles." She clicked a jagged piece of cardboard into place.

I smiled, enjoying the zany antics with my best friend. "Yeah, that's enough for tonight, let's finish this instead."

After Sabrina left, I tidied up and let Ruby out one last time before heading to bed. Once there, I pulled the covers up under my chin. As I lay there a realization washed over me. Bryan could possibly be the one who sent me the letter. It made sense – he was just too shy to tell me how he felt.

I covered my face with my hands and tried but failed to shut out any thoughts about Bryan. Not him, please, anyone but him.

I had damage control to do. I had to get Bryan off my back and get out of his heart.

CHAPTER 14

Reggie

Last night, I tossed and turned, reliving the mess I had made of my marriage. I've lost sleep every night since Betty left me. I can't live with myself, and I can't live without her. What a mess I'm in!

When the clock finally struck 6 a.m., I decided to give up on trying to get any sleep. I wrapped my worn housecoat around me and headed for the stairs. As soon as my bare feet touched the cold, hardwood floor I remembered leaving my slippers in the living room. Gingerly, I made my way to the fireplace. It took an eternity to light a fire and to feel some relief when the amber glow I had feebly started finally erupted into crackling red flames.

Next stop was the kitchen to make some coffee. Betty always made my morning brew, but now that I was alone, I couldn't figure out even how to turn the damn coffee machine on. Instead of learning to use it, I had given up and bought some instant coffee to fuel me. No need to fuss with any fancy drip.

When I turned around to get the cream from the fridge, Bruce leapt onto the counter with something brown firmly clutched in his jaw. The morning light hadn't yet pooled in the kitchen. I turned on the overhead light and gasped at what he had.

"You little bugger! You scared me half to death!" Surprised by my reaction, he dropped a live mouse onto the floor. My instinct was to jump, and I ended up hitting my back against the counter. I yelled at him, but he was so proud of his conquest that he just purred back at me.

"At least you finally caught something. I guess that's a start," I surrendered. A pat on the head and some kibble in his bowl was my reward for this half-assed feline hunter. Then, I grabbed a broom and tried to shoo the dazed mouse out of the house. I didn't have the heart to kill it, even if I demanded that from the cat.

I pulled my cellphone out of my pocket and ran my thumb across the screen, awakening the device from its slumber. There was one person I desperately wanted to tell about the cat's hunting skills, but that person wasn't currently speaking to me. I felt a pang of sadness in my chest; I tried to rub my sternum to ease the pain, but it didn't help.

Maybe Maggie was awake. I decided to send her a text to tell her about the morning's events.

Dad: You'll never believe what the cat did. Guess!

I stirred the instant coffee crystals until they dissolved in the hot water and stood waiting, staring at the phone for a response from my daughter, but nothing came.

A few minutes passed, and still there was no reply from Maggie. I took a sip of my coffee, and my face puckered in distaste. Too many crystals! This stuff tasted awful. I made my way to the sink and poured the sludge down the drain.

I checked my phone again. Nothing! Maybe Maggie was still asleep. I shouldn't bother her, but I convinced myself that if she were late for work, I should send another message to wake her up.

Dad: The cat got a damn mouse!
Dad: He let go of it in the house!

Still no word. Then, suddenly, three little dots appeared and vanished just as quickly as they first appeared on the screen.

Dad: Can you believe it?

I was grasping at straws for attention. If I were being honest with myself, I felt very lonely lately. "Geez! When did I become so needy?" I grumbled. I could hardly recognize myself anymore.

I set my phone down and took a sip of my second attempt at making coffee. I winced when the bitter taste hit my tongue. Still too many crystals. It tasted awful! I made a mental note to head down to *Bean There, Done That* when it opened. Marnie always made a good cup of joe. I needed to get out of the house anyway and pop down to see Lou.

Just then, my phone came to life. I nearly had a heart attack.

"Hello?" I asked with some annoyance, anticipating yet another telemarketer calling from an unknown number, though I would probably welcome anyone to talk to.

"Hey, Dad. It's me."

My body relaxed as the realization set in that the call was from my pride and joy. "Maggie, love. How are you?" I wondered if she could sense my smile.

"I'm fine, how are you? Everything okay?" She sounded distressed. The last thing I wanted was for my daughter to worry about me even if I wasn't okay.

I wanted to tell Maggie how lonely I felt and how much I missed her mother, but instead I said, "Of course. Everything here is just fine. Bruce gave me a good chuckle this morning. I thought you'd appreciate an update."

I heard a snicker on the other end of the receiver. "So, you like him now?" Sounds beeped in the background, and I could faintly hear chattering.

"I like your fur brother just fine." I winced as soon as the words slipped out of my mouth. Betty always referred to Bruce as our 'son' and told Maggie that Bruce was her 'brother.' I would complain about it, reminding her that the cat wasn't biologically related to us, but Betty would insist that you don't have to be related to be family. And, I knew that she wasn't wrong.

"I'm glad he's keeping you company." I imagined her smile at the other end of the line.

"How are you? Where are you?" I asked quizzically.

"I'm at work. We aren't allowed to make calls on our cellphones, so I'm at the nurses' station calling you." I could hear her clicking on a keyboard.

"That explains the unknown number." Mystery solved.

"Are you sure that you're okay?" Maggie knew me better than I knew myself at times. I felt a bit choked up when I answered her.

I felt tears forming. "I've been better," my voice cracked.

"Oh, Dad." Her words wrapped around me like a hug. "I'm sorry."

"I'm sorry, too." I looked up at the ceiling, willing the tears to stay in their ducts. No one needed any waterworks now.

"Have you tried again lately?" Maggie asked. She was always following up with me to see how things were going between her mom and me.

"Every week, but nothing. She isn't budging." I exhaled my frustrations. I wished that Betty would at least talk to me.

I cleared my throat. "Have you heard from her?" I asked, feeling hopeful.

There was a long pause on the other end. Perhaps the call was dropped, or the boss was making their rounds.

"Maggie?" I asked, concerned.

"I'm here, Dad." She reluctantly continued. "No, she refuses to talk about you to me when I call."

"Figures. She's stubborn."

"Just like you," she replied without hesitation.

I grimaced at Maggie's words. She wasn't wrong about that.

"Anyways, let's talk about Christmas. When are you coming home?"

"Dad, I can't. It's my turn to work Christmas this year." Her voice sounded small. I couldn't help but feel disappointed. She was right; she had come home last year for the holiday. I wished she'd come home this year because I didn't want to be alone. Why was I being so selfish?

Sensing my disappointment she suggested, "I could come up for a few days before Christmas." I bit my stubbled lip, contemplating the offer. "We could watch old movies and work on the car," she added. My spirits lifted, if only for a moment.

This was not the family holiday I had imagined. Betty, Maggie, and I always spent some part of the holiday together. Was this my life now? Were we going to become one of those broken families where the kid had to decide who to spend each holiday with? This was not the life I had envisioned, not even as an old man.

With one final attempt to please her grumpy old dad, she threw out an unusual invitation, "Or you can come here to visit for New Year's Eve! We could explore the city – you decide," she added. I knew she was doing her best to cheer me up.

"Sure, sweetheart." I felt heartache spread through my body, exploding like a nuclear bomb. I needed to be brave for my little girl, even though she wasn't so little anymore. "That would be great." I forced a smile, despite feeling broken inside.

I was trying my best to move forward in life.

I said goodbye to my only daughter and hung up the phone. I decided to try to maintain my routine as best as I could. I had a shower and dressed. I scattered birdseed and shooed the squirrels away from the feeder.

When the clock struck 10 a.m., I decided to head into town. But first, I had one last call to make. I still couldn't get used to the cellphone Maggie gave me for Christmas last year. She also purchased one of those family plans for Betty and me. Betty was always texting up a storm to Maggie or her sister. I, for one, struggled to type on that little screen. Because my fat fingers could never hit the keys quite right, whenever I wanted to make a call, I'd use the house phone— not many people have one of those left.

As usual, after three rings, my call went to voicemail. "Hi, it's Betty. I can't answer the phone right now, but I'll get back to you when I can. Love you!"

My stomach dropped. That love certainly wasn't for me. I stood tall, puffed out my chest, and delivered my news. "Betty, it's me – your husband." She should know who I am – unless she found another mate.

"I hope you are having a nice day, with…" I could barely say her name, "Sophia." Sophia was Betty's younger sister.

I soldiered on. "Maggie won't be coming home for Christmas, but we're making plans for the holiday. Perhaps you can return my call to see when we might all be able to get together. It would be nice to spend time with our-" I was interrupted by three beeps and an automated voice reminding me I had 30 seconds to finish my voicemail. Damn technology, "daughter," I continued. "I hope you enjoyed the roses and the stuffed teddy bear. It's been very popular at *The Shrinking Violet*. Talk soon." I took a deep breath to ground myself after I hung up the phone.

Damn, I should have told her about Bruce! She would've gotten a kick out of that. I almost picked up the phone to call her back, but I stopped myself. I didn't want to seem desperate. After all, she hadn't responded to any of my communications yet. I'd save that news for when she called me back.

Just as I was about to put on my boots and leave, the doorbell rang aggressively three times. It had better not be another door-to-door salesperson. I wasn't interested in upgrading my cable package or whatever else they might be peddling!

With an irritated sigh, I stomped down the hallway and swung the door open before the bell could ring a fourth time. I was confronted by a group of snot-nosed child carolers. Didn't they know I was about to leave? I wasn't interested in their nonsense.

I tried to wave off the carolers, signalling that I had to go, but that didn't seem to stop them. Against my wishes, Father Erikson led the choir in my front yard. I was too distracted by more unwanted Christmas mail that I had just retrieved from my box to ask him to stop. One clumsy-looking kid stood too close to my coveted rose bush. Betty would kill me if that bush got crushed; it was her favourite.

Momentarily, I was transported back to last summer. I pictured stepping out of the front door and sitting in the creaky brown rocking chair on the porch. Betty always sat on the front steps so she could admire the garden. Every flower was like her own child; she took tender, loving care of each plant. She'd drink her morning coffee and watch over her garden for hours, waiting for it to do something magical. I'd sit in the chair, rocking and studying her smile. I'd do anything to make that lady happy. I loved the way she sat there, admiring the pink petals.

I came back to my senses; memories of Betty would have to wait. I tried to wave the kid away from her prized rosebush, but he didn't seem to get the hint.

Neither did Father Erikson who continued to flail his arms and encourage his carolers, "Ready, everyone! In 3, 2, 1..." And, in chaotic unison, the small humans began to sing their painful rendition of a classic Christmas song.

The last thing I wanted was to stand in the cold and listen to this chaos. It was truly awful. If only I had my earplugs from work handy. Irritation washed over me, and my tumultuous emotions morphed into roaring waves of anger. I needed to get away. These kids were stressing me out with their noise.

In that moment, I felt as if I was stuck in a time machine, tormented by my memories, tortured by my mistakes. I was transported back to the night we were married. Christmas music was playing on the car radio. Betty sat beside me, her white wedding dress blooming around her. She was singing the same song at the top of her lungs as we headed out of town to Niagara Falls, the honeymoon capital of Canada. Back then, it was all we could afford for a holiday; money was tight, and we were saving for a house and, soon after that, a child. However, Betty always clung to the dream of going to Hawaii someday for a proper honeymoon.

I remember looking over at her as she sang off-key. I remember squeezing her hand, trying to savour the special moment. She looked so happy. We were so happy, back then! But right now, I couldn't let myself get caught up in nostalgia. My wife wasn't speaking to me, and I didn't have time for this nonsense.

"Kids, can you please?" I began with a polite yet somewhat hostile tone. I rubbed my hands together to self-soothe; that's one of the things mentioned in those self-help books I've been trying to read, but this hippy-dippy self-care approach wasn't working. I could feel my blood pressure rising.

Much to my chagrin, the children continued singing. Father Erikson turned around to smile and nod at me while he simultaneously led them into the chorus. I desperately longed to let him know that his roadshow needed some fine-tuning.

"Kids- I need to get going," I said a little louder, trying to talk over them without yelling. I didn't want a bunch of angry parents filling up my voicemail. However, my pleas fell on deaf ears. Even though with every note of the singing, I saw flashes of Betty's smile, I needed the madness to end.

"Kids!" I bellowed. My voice boomed across the yard, startling a pair of cardinals in one of the barren trees on my front lawn. The frightened children abruptly stopped singing. My nostrils flared with irritation. I tried to steady myself. Father Erikson stood with his mouth gaping open. "Kids, please leave. I don't want to hear any more caroling!"

I turned on my heels, headed inside and slammed the door as hard as I could. Don't people know when to stop? I leaned back against the door and steadied myself. I placed my hand over my heart. The muscular organ pumped hard against my ribcage. I was relieved that I still had a heart. So much for self-improvement, I huffed at my flaws. Maybe I was still that grumpy old man Betty complained that I was.

As soon as I caught my breath, I heard a rumble from overhead. This was followed by muffled screams. My first thought was that the garage roof that I had neglected to repair despite Betty's many warnings had collapsed on my precious car. I swung open the door in a panic, ready to leap into action. Thank my lucky stars the roof was still intact. However, all the snow that had built up had cascaded in an avalanche onto the unsuspecting carolers, no doubt the consequence of my having slammed the door so hard.

A figure rose from the snow, his chest heaving. Father Erikson called out exasperated, "You kids, okay?" He brushed the snow off his face and scowled at me.

I admit, I was relieved that none of the kids were hurt, but at the same time, I feared that they might pelt my house with snowballs. They didn't. Instead, they brushed off the snow from their multi-coloured snowsuits and headed down the walkway intent, probably, on annoying another hapless homeowner down the street.

I shrugged my shoulders and headed back inside.

CHAPTER 15

Wyatt

I spent most of last night tossing and turning. Maybe it was Rachel's awful sound machine that she claimed helped her to maintain her Zen attitude. That was probably some sort of hoax that people with too much money bought into. Worse still, I couldn't get what Reggie said at the hardware store out of my head...divorce. Were marriages destined for that doomed fate?

You hardly enter marriage thinking about it ending, or I'd hope not, anyway. No doubt some people get married before they've had a chance to discover who they are as individuals. Society has this unfortunate tendency to pressure people into marrying while they're young, so that your parent can walk you down the aisle and you can start a family. Some couples who buy into this idea grow apart or refuse to allow the other space to grow. Tragedy makes it difficult for others to move on, and they end up falling apart. I'm sure there are other reasons why people break up, but their stories were none of my business.

In my family, my dad never even managed to contact my mom to sign the divorce papers. Dad regarded himself as divorced but never elaborated on why my mom left; eventually, we just stopped discussing her.

When I reached the shop this morning, I was rather grumpy. I was tired. My shirt was wrinkled. I hadn't even had a cup of coffee yet. I was miserable. I placed all of the blame for my mood at Rachel's feet. Rachel, my sister from hell.

At breaktime, I decided to head over to *Bean There, Done That*. Marnie sure knew how to make a good cup of coffee. I needed that java to flow like lava through my veins in order to get through the rest of the day.

When I pulled up, it looked like a full house. Bob Collins was seated in a booth with his son, Derek, who had come to visit for the holidays. I had gone to high school with him, but didn't know him well enough to necessarily go over and start up a conversation; he had been one of the cool kids in school, and part of me still felt a little intimidated by him. He was, however, whipped by Naomi Weir when they dated in school – so maybe he wasn't so bad after all. Thankfully, he had escaped her grasp and married some woman he met at university.

As I crossed the tiled floor, I passed behind Rich O'Neil who was working on a crossword puzzle at the counter as part of his morning routine. Usually, when he had completed the puzzle, he'd go back to work where he'd criticize his high school employees for not stocking the shelves properly. He operated that store like a drill sergeant. At least the store looked nice!

The café was scattered with others I didn't quite recognize, but then a lone soul, Reggie, who was sitting by himself, caught my eye. His head hung over a steaming cup of coffee. He looked as if he hated life. I thought about chatting him up later, after I got my order filled. I was desperate for caffeine!

And then there was Marnie, my Patron Saint of Coffee, working behind the counter. She was filling orders of bacon and eggs, toast with jam, and freshly baked scones. Damn, it smelled good in here. I ran out of the house again this morning to avoid more family bonding time with my sister, and didn't get my breakfast in my great escape. My best hope was that Bryan would take her out so that I could avoid more sibling rivalry under the guise of bonding when I returned home. Putting this out of my mind, I gave the gentlemen in the café a nod, made my way through the crowd and found a stool at the counter.

Marnie rounded the counter, patted me on the shoulder after I took my seat, and started refilling coffee for her customers. "Thanks, Marnie," Reggie grumbled. "I needed this," he sucked in a breath. I could almost hear him sinking into the upholstery.

"You're welcome, hon." Marnie's gold rings clinked against the glass coffee pot as she floated through the room. She sprinkled love wherever she went.

"What can I get you, Wy?" There was only a select group of people – Marnie, Sabrina, and my dad - who dared to call me that. She'd always been a bit of a mother figure for me.

"Coffee," I replied, mimicking a zombie, "I feel dead inside." I dragged my hands down my face, my eyes dry.

Marnie smiled, the wrinkles around her eyes crinkling in response to my joke. "That bad, huh?" She reached under the counter for a uniform white mug. I watched as coffee flowed like a waterfall into the cup. She handed me a bowl of creamers; she knew how I liked my coffee. "Rachel bugging you with all that sisterly love?"

"How'd you know she was home?" News travelled fast around here so I shouldn't have been surprised by her question.

Marnie's face flushed. "Oh, Lou was in here yesterday and mentioned it," she brushed me and the conversation off.

I nodded. That made sense. Dad loved his coffee, too. He was even talking about changing the complimentary sludge we passed off as coffee in the store to a *Bean There, Done That* coffee alternative.

Marnie roasted and ground her own beans; she was a miracle woman, a coffee aficionado.

"Marnie," I called her name from my slumped position at the counter, "I've got a question for you." With each sip, I felt more human and ready to ask the questions that had been playing on repeat in my mind.

"Shoot, hon." She leaned across the counter and rubbed my hand.

"What do you think about marriage?" I bit the inside of my cheek. I wasn't looking for another person to pressure me into marriage, but I wanted some honest answers.

Marnie looked playfully taken aback. "Oh, sweetie, I'm a little old for you, don't you think?" She asked as she winked at me.

My face reddened. "That's not what I meant," I said softly, feeling slightly embarrassed myself.

Marnie pulled back from the counter with a feigned shocked face. "How dare you? I'm a catch!" She grabbed a coffee pot and started her rounds refilling coffee for her customers again. I sat there, contemplating whether I wanted to keep this conversation flowing.

"Why do you ask?" She gave me a sly smile when she returned to the counter. "Are you thinking about popping the question?" Her eyes grew wide with excitement.

I shrugged, because truthfully, I didn't know what I wanted to do. I felt as if, with everyone pressuring me to ask Sabrina to marry me, I might as well find out what people thought about marriage to see if it was the right decision for me.

"If you want my opinion," Rich offered. To be clear, I hadn't asked Rich for his opinion. "Marriage was the best decision I ever made, next to taking over the family's grocery store." He folded his crossword puzzle. "Work was made even better when my wife took over the baking department. Now I get to see Beth all day, every day."

Out of the corner of my eye, I could see Reggie lean over, as if to absorb the conversation. Even Bob and Derek stopped their conversation to look over. I felt as if all eyes were on me.

"Doesn't that get a little annoying?" Reggie interjected, his voice flat.

"What?" Rich spun around in his seat to face Reggie. "I love Beth. She's my world." It was impossible to miss the twinkle in Rich's eye.

Reggie came back with an embarrassed retort. "I just mean, all day seems like a lot, doesn't it?" he said, trying to pivot the conversation to a more positive mood. I could sense he was miserable, and it wasn't just for lack of coffee.

"Well, maybe, but she's usually too busy whipping up pies or cakes." He thought to himself. I like knowing she's close by, and if I miss her smile, I just pop by the baking department and then carry on with my day." He smiled to himself.

Reggie grunted in return; it was hard to read that man. Why had he been so crabby lately?

Seeing Sabrina every day, all day, might be a little distracting, but I know that I appreciated her coming to the shop with the mail. Seeing her just made the workday that much easier.

From the chair behind me Derek offered, "My wife is supportive. She's been my rock through grad school," he sighed happily.

"I didn't know you were in grad school, that's awesome," I congratulated him. He had always made the honour roll in high school, so I shouldn't have been surprised by that accomplishment.

"Thanks," he said sheepishly, as if grad school was something to be embarrassed about. "When the days are long and the workload is hard, Grace is always there for me. She's supported me since day one," he held up a finger.

Bob chimed in, "She's a wonderful woman." Bob raised his mug to his son.

"I'm lucky. We've been married about six months now." He looked down at his gold wedding ring. "She's a great wife."

"I'm happy for you," I nodded towards Derek.

Sabrina was a supportive partner; she never said a negative thing when I chose to stay in Mercer to work for my dad. She had the chance to move to Toronto for a job, but she decided against it. She said she was happy coming back to Mercer after school and working here. I hoped she didn't move back because of me; I would never want to be the one to squash her dreams.

"Supporting each other, huh." Reggie quietly murmured. I looked over at him and wrinkled my eyebrows. What was going on with him?

"That, and humour. You gotta have a sense of humour," Bob added, then took a swig of his coffee. He raised his mug to Marnie, signalling that he was ready for more.

"That's right, laughter is key," Rich echoed. "There will be good days, and bad days, that's for sure – like a recession!" The men in the shop muttered in agreement.

"My wife and I try not to take life too seriously," Bob added. "We've had our fair share of ups and downs. Through those times, you have to laugh." Everyone nodded, almost in unison.

Sabrina and I felt as if we had our own language – we'd look at each other and laugh. We didn't even have to say anything.

"Gosh, I didn't know I was hosting the *Mercer Men's Support Group*. I should start charging for entry!" Marnie laughed. "Glad you fellas were more help to Wy than I was." Marnie placed freshly baked brownies into the showcase, and the scent of chocolate wafted through the air. I motioned to her for a brownie.

Just then, the conversation in the café was broken when my dad entered. "Marnie, how's it going?" his voice boomed. Whenever he saw Marnie, his smile lit up the entire room. I wondered what put my dad in such a good mood.

"What can I get you, love?" The two of them were lost in a trance, as if no one else was in the room.

Wait a second. Love? Marnie usually called everyone 'hon' or 'sweetie', didn't she? I was too deep in thought to see everyone else around the café make knowing eyes at each other.

"Lou, the usual?" Marnie continued, not missing a beat.

"Absolutely," Dad clasped his hands together and took a seat beside me.

"Son, don't stay too long. We have a fender bender coming in, and that's going to take up our afternoon."

I put my head on the counter. Not more work! I was already exhausted, but I knew that I needed to soldier on, even if I didn't want to. "Got it," I gave my dad the thumbs up.

After his to-go cup was filled, I caught him as he flashed a wink and smiled at Marnie before he bolted out the door.

"What about you, Marnie?" I took a bite of my brownie. "Have you ever been married?"

"Oh, not me, Wy, you know that." Marnie seemed flustered, certainly not her usual self.

"I know, but you never wanted to get married?" Marnie was a catch. It surprised me that she was single for as long as I've known her.

"I never saw a need to." Her smile fell, "I was busy working and taking care of my mother. I had other things going on in my life." She swept crumbs off the counter, avoiding eye contact with me. "Marriage wasn't really in the cards for me."

"But, would you ever want to marry?" I persisted.

"If the right man came along, maybe," she said with a coy smile. "But, right now, I'm living my best life."

After I emptied my second cup of coffee, I got up to leave. When I turned around, Reggie was hot on my heels.

"Wyatt, can I talk to you for a minute?" he asked.

"What's up?" Maybe now I'd find out what had him in such a foul mood.

"I wanted to apologize for yesterday. Things have been a bit rocky at home." He said awkwardly.

"I'm sorry to hear that." I hated to hear people were going through tough times.

"The truth is, I've been feeling sour about marriage, because Betty left me a couple of months ago."

"What?" I said, taken aback. "I'm so sorry,"

"That's okay, son. I'm trying to win her back, but so far, no luck." He shook his head in frustration. "But I won't give up."

"Let me know if I can do anything for you, Reggie." And I meant that. I'd help anyone out if they needed it.

"I appreciate that." Reggie smiled and patted me on the back. "Love is a beautiful thing," he sighed, likely missing his wife. "Sabrina is a special woman. You two seem happy. Whatever you decide will be the right decision. Trust your gut." Reggie headed back to his truck and zoomed out of sight. I stood outside the café, taking in what he had shared.

I finally felt as if I could breathe a sigh of relief. If I were to tell you the truth, I had almost asked Sabrina to marry me once, but I chickened out. I had let Rachel get in the way, and I've regretted it ever since.

CHAPTER 16

Dana

Of all people, I asked myself, why Bryan? What more could there be to this story than the events of today? Could this mystery reach back as far as the sixth grade when Wyatt and I received invitations to 12-year-old Naomi's birthday party? What we both anticipated would be a heavenly experience was more like a living hell, as I remember it.

She was one of the most popular girls in school. An invitation to her Christmas-themed birthday celebration was a guaranteed shoo-in to a seat at the cool kids' cafeteria table next year in junior high. We couldn't believe our luck at being included.

"What do I even get a girl for her birthday?" Wyatt whined. His dad had given us a lift north, to the nearest mall, to go shopping the weekend before the party. His ulterior motive was gift shopping for Wyatt and his little sister, Rachel. We sifted through accessories at the local teen fad store. I was bemused watching him pick up fuzzy journals and pens with giant lips on them, inspecting them, wondering why anyone would even buy these things. I think, at one point, that I heard him mutter "What the hell is this?" when he picked up an electronic fortune cookie.

I sighed and went on with my own birthday gift shopping. I inspected some silver earrings and weighed them against my option of a 'best friends' necklace. If I wanted a seat at the popular table, I had to be strategic.

Naomi and I had been partners for a science project the previous fall. Because she was so involved in other school clubs and activities, I didn't mind working on the project for both of us. She was super happy when we got an 'A' on the project. My hope was that this would win me points with her and that I would gain acceptance into her coveted circle of friends.

I was wrong. She used me, as popular kids often do. I should've known better, but I desperately wanted to fit in.

On the night of the birthday party, Wyatt's Dad drove us to Naomi's house on the outskirts of town. It was dark when our headlights lit up the long driveway. We were greeted by flashing woodland creatures covered in white twinkling lights, tall pine trees decked with multicoloured lights eventually fading up in the night sky, rotating elves making presents and the grand finale, Santa waving from his sleigh led by a crew of wooden reindeer. "These people have money," Wyatt's dad said a little too loudly. I looked down at my foil-wrapped gift, hoping that I had made the right choice.

I snapped out of it when a cold gust of wind startled me. "Thanks!" Wyatt called out as he slammed the car door shut.

"Thanks, Mr. Greene!" I echoed. Nervously, I followed Wyatt to the front door. Naomi's grandmother, with whom she lived, answered the door and took our winter coats so we could join the others.

The evening started out fine. It was the usual pizza party with presents piled high on the counter. This time, however, the latest blockbuster movie was replaced with music videos, and instead of 'pin the tail on the donkey', it was 'truth or dare' or an even worse fate.

But first, it came time to open gifts. Naomi tore through the presents without care. It looked like a little kid's Christmas morning aftermath with gifts and torn wrapping paper littering the living room. Not a shred of carpet could be seen. When she came to my gift, my heart stopped beating. Naomi looked down at the little box and pouted. My gift was smaller in comparison to the makeup and purses that others had gifted her. With a quick shrug, she ripped into the paper. Her eyes lit up when she saw the little black cardboard box.

"Dana, you shouldn't have!" she fussed. When she wiggled the lid of the box open, panic took over my body. Would she like it? Confusion spread over her face, and what I thought was a smirk. "Dana, you *shouldn't have*," she giggled and showed the box to Tamara Adams, my worst nightmare at school. I felt totally and utterly humiliated. They were making fun of me. I should've gone with the earrings.

After a while, Naomi's grandmother went to her room for a rest. I guess looking after 25 pre-pubescent kids was a handful. As soon as her grandmother told us to "Holler if you need anything," she made her way up the steps. Her exit was a signal to her mischievous grand spawn that the tone of the party was about to change. Naomi wasted no time in seizing the opportunity to do just that.

So, you're probably thinking, what does this party have to do with me and Bryan? Slow your roll, I'm getting to it.

The mood lighting changed, and for many of the partygoers, so did their emotions. "Let's play 'seven minutes in heaven'! Who's in?" asked Naomi. Several of us looked around at each other panic stricken. I knew that other kids in my class were dating each other. When I think back, what did that even mean at that age? Some of us didn't have any desire yet to hold hands with a boy, let alone kiss them. At that age, I hardly had any interest in any boy. Sure, I listened to the popular rock band at the time, but that didn't mean that I wanted to kiss them! EW!

And yet, here I was, on the brink of becoming a teenager, whether I was ready or not.

Naomi stood from her cross-legged position, brushing off the excess glitter and lingering ribbon onto the floor. "So, who wants to go in the closet first?" she asked. "I'd go first, but Derek and I already make out." She leaned down and gave her pimple-faced, brace-laced boyfriend a noisy kiss. I, for one, was aghast- I did *not* want to do that!

She crept around the makeshift circle we'd created when we watched her open her gifts. I thought I was going to pass out from anxiety and the flashing lights from her tinsel-covered tree. She lurked behind us, selecting her victim. She stopped at Bryan who smiled sheepishly as he devoured his third slice of birthday cake. "You're first!" Naomi excitedly informed him.

"Cool! What do we do?" he smiled. Green icing stained his teeth. Naomi groaned a little and shifted into a menacing giggle.

"You'll find out." Naomi looked around the room to see who'd be joining him. I didn't know if it was the one too many pieces of candy cane fudge or the thought of being locked up with green teeth that made me want to hurl. My stomach flipped when her eyes rested on mine.

A sinister smile spread across the birthday girl's face. "Dana, how about you join him?" I knew from the moment she opened her gift that her heart was ten times too small, even though I should've known better when we did our project together.

"Oh no, someone else can go first, I'll wait," I stuttered. My face flushed scarlet. I searched for Wyatt to save me, and I later learned he had locked himself in the bathroom to escape this horrid game. That, and he was hiding from Tamara, whom he suspected had a crush on him.

"Come on, it's my birthday!" She twirled her curls around her little finger. "Do it for me, it's my birthday after all, *bestie*." There was an orchestra of stifled laughter from around the darkened room. I knew that I had no choice in the matter. This was probably the first and only time in several years that I'd kiss a boy. I didn't want my first kiss to be with him, but I wanted to be friends with Naomi.

Thinking back, why did it matter so much? What did I really care about her? Hindsight is 20/20, as they say.

Before I knew it, I was being led into the coat closet in the front hallway with Bryan. All I remember is hearing inaudible voices explaining the rules and being shoved into the dark space with green teeth. Those few minutes felt like an eternity. I could feel the heavy winter coats press against my back. With every movement, they shuffled loudly against me. I was so close to him that I could feel his warm breath, sweet from cake and spicy from nachos, against my face. Later in life, we'd both learn the importance of mints when it came time to kiss other people.

"So," he tried to play it cool.

"So," I offered back.

He gulped nervously. In the darkness, I could make out the lines of his face and the twinkle in his eyes, faintly lit by the front hallway lighting. Chuckling voices from the living room reminded us of the time.

"So, do you want to kiss?" Bryan mustered. He reached his sweaty hand out and gently took mine. He was making his move, might as well. The truth was I didn't want to kiss him, and he sensed that, "Or not. We could totally just talk." I sighed with relief. He still held onto my hand which I didn't mind. For the next two minutes, he regaled me with a whispered story about his new bearded dragon. Bryan was always a talker, and he never grew out of that.

"Sixty seconds!" Naomi bellowed. I could hear creaking outside the door, likely where she stood hovering and eavesdropping.

"I hope you're having fun. Maybe we can sit together on the bus next week and I can tell you more about my dragon." I smiled, thinking that Bryan was so sweet to me. He didn't push when he realized I didn't want to kiss him, and he made me feel comfortable with him in an uncomfortable situation.

"Sure," I said. "That would be cool." And just like that, I did the most unexpected thing: I leaned in and kissed Bryan on the cheek. When I drew back, I saw, in slow motion, his jaw drop, and his eyes widen. Before another word could be spoken, the doors of the closet flew open. For a brief second there was a bright light, and then a figure loomed over us darkening the doorway.

It wasn't Naomi, but her grandmother who demanded to know, "What's going on here?" We were hustled out into the hallway by our Christmas-themed sweater collars. In the hustle and bustle, the garland and mistletoe that hung overhead fell on Bryan's head adding to his embarrassment.

"Grams! Be cool. It's my birthday!" Naomi begged.

"I expected you to behave under my roof!" She flicked on all the lights to make sure there were no other shenanigans.

"We were only playing a game. Right, Dana?"

The last thing I wanted was to get into trouble. I eyed Wyatt, who had emerged from his hiding place. He shrugged his shoulders, not offering much in the way of support.

"*Right,* Dana?" Naomi crossed her arms, her eyes burning holes in me.

"Right." I croaked.

But grandma was not appeased, nor was she a happy camper in any sense of the word. "The party's over. Call your parents. You're all going home," she insisted.

Thank goodness, I thought. I was saved by the Christmas monster.

When Wyatt's dad showed up, he asked us how the party was and wondered why it was over before the scheduled pickup time of 10 p.m. "We ran out of food," Wyatt offered. A lame excuse, but his dad didn't contest it.

As we started to reverse out of the driveway, I wondered what it might have been like if I had had a few more uninterrupted seconds in the closet with Bryan. I saw his face one last time as we headed down the driveway. He sheepishly waved to me, hopeful that we'd sit on the bus together the following week, but we didn't.

Wyatt and I never made it to the cool kids' table. To be honest, I didn't talk to Bryan again for the rest of the year out of embarrassment for kissing him. It wasn't until I came back to Mercer after college that he struck up any type of conversation with me. Bryan was always such a good guy. I didn't deserve him then, and I sure didn't deserve him now.

CHAPTER 17

Reggie

Enough was enough. I decided to visit Betty, her sister be damned! It was time to talk some sense into Betty and bring her home where she belonged.

I rummaged through the drawers until I found my best sweater - the black and white one that Betty knitted for me a few years ago. She was so proud of it. I tried to wear it on every occasion I could, to please her. I never had the heart to tell her it was a little too tight in the tummy, and that the wool scratched the exposed skin at the nape of my neck. Ah, the things you do for love. Rather, the things I *did* for love.

I fumbled in the bathroom to slick back my grey hair, just the way Betty liked it whenever we dressed to go out. I set the comb down and took a long, hard look in the mirror and caught the reflection of my large, sad eyes. I looked away, ashamed.

With renewed determination, I gripped the rounded corners of the laminate countertop and squeezed the edges, sending a dull pain through my palms. I wasn't the same old Reggie anymore; I was on my way to being a new man – one that Betty deserved. A man doesn't change overnight, but I was doing my best the last little while.

I took one last look at my reflection and nodded knowingly to myself. "You can do it," I whispered. I was learning the importance of positive self-talk, or whatever that gibberish was.

I was going to pull out all the stops after my weeks of failed gifting to Betty. If I looked nice when I showed up today, surely that would be the icing on the cake, and she'd take me back.

I'd been mustering up the courage for weeks to go and see her, but every time I tried to leave, I'd stall at my front door. I had been afraid of her answer. Since Betty left me, she's been staying with her sister. At least I knew where she was, and for all I knew, she hadn't found another man to shack up with yet.

With my newfound confidence I walked into the kitchen, yanked Bruce's food container from the shelf and dumped two cups of kibble out for him. He looked up at me with wide eyes, as if he had just won the cat jackpot. I swear his purrs were amplified as he dashed over and chowed down. The name tag on his collar clanged against the dish as he feasted. I was optimistic that I wouldn't be coming home for a bit and wanted to make sure that the little bugger didn't perish while I was gone.

I wasted no time getting into the truck. I pulled out of the driveway, revved the engine and headed out of town.

In the hour it took for me to drive to Betty's hideaway, I had a lot of time to reflect. I reflected on the work I had done to improve myself, all the books and those podcast things Maggie had sent me to listen to. I even watched some of those television hosts who tried to empower men to connect with their feminine side. I found it hokey at first, but I'd do whatever I could to win Betty back. I wanted to become the man I knew I could become, for her sake and mine.

Self-improvement wasn't the only thing I had been doing to win back my wife. I had been showering her with gifts – gestures of love,

I think they call them. I was pretty sure that all the purchases I had been making at Dana's shop had earned me shares in her business. She's been very helpful to a hopeless man like me with all her gift suggestions for Betty. Maggie said I should regularly shower my wife with affection. I thought that's what I had been doing all these years, but I guess I didn't do it as often as Betty would've liked. Maggie even sent me those text things with pictures of whatever she thought her mom would enjoy. She encouraged me to keep trying to win her back. Even Juan from the lumber yard got into the act; he would drop off parcels for Betty on his lumber deliveries. I kept telling people that she was looking after her sick sister, but that was a lie because I just couldn't deal with that detestable woman.

I slowed down as I entered the village limits. I took the old, familiar twists and turns through the suburbs until I reached Betty's hiding place.

Once I parked the truck at the end of the driveway, I closed my eyes and took a few deep breaths to calm my nerves. Hopefully, this was it. Betty would finally forgive me and come home. I did my best to ground myself, that's what Maggie called it. Then, I opened the truck door but before I had a chance to set one foot on the ground, I encountered my worst nemesis.

"Haven't you learned to take a hint?" Sophia, Betty's sister, made my body have a visceral reaction every time I heard her voice. I equated it with the sound of nails on a chalkboard. I tried to force a smile. I knew I'd have to fight this gnarly, old dragon if I was to reclaim my princess.

"Sophia, so nice to see you as well." With as much determination as I could muster, I set both feet on the ground, closed the truck door shut and made my way through the freshly fallen snow. Before I could even get to the front door, she moved to block my way.

"Not so fast, screwball." Sophia placed her arthritic hand on my chest. It took everything I had in me not to react to her. I'd love to break her gnarled fingers, but I knew that there would be consequences.

This wasn't the first time Sophia tried to get between Betty and me. No, there must've been half a dozen times that Sophia tried to interfere with our relationship. Betty and I almost didn't get married because of her, but that's a story for another time.

The cold winter air had fogged the edges of her thick glasses, but I could still see her squinting, judging me with her cataract-laden eyes. "She doesn't want to see you."

I readied for battle. "Is that so?"

"It is." She looked me up and down with obvious contempt.

I had the feeling that she wasn't going to budge. I decided to call her bluff and try to make my way past her. She scolded me with the same disapproving sound one might make towards a child as she wagged a finger in my face.

I took a deep breath and tried again. I tried to be tactful. "Please, Sophia. I want to see my wife." If I had to beg, I had to beg. Whatever it took to get to Betty, I'd do it.

"I said no," she huffed. "Betty doesn't want to see you." She took a pack of cigarettes out of her coat pocket and slid a thin white stick out of the package.

"But Sophia, she's my wife." I held a hand to my chest. I could feel the ache through my body. I couldn't face another day without Betty.

"You messed up big time talking to her the way you did." She turned her back and cupped her hands, bringing embers to life. She took a long drag as she gave me time to feel badly for how I had spoken to my wife.

"I know and trust me." I was in agony. "I feel bad about it every single day." Sophia was sticking the gears to me, and I could feel the pain.

"Ha!" Sophia blew a mouthful of dreadful smoke on my face. "Good one." She leaned forward. Steadying herself with the feeble railing, she sneered, "You should feel bad."

The emotions brewing in my chest created a tug of war: I was devastated that my wife didn't want to see me, and I felt angry that this troll was blocking the bridge to forgiveness between me and Betty.

This felt like a losing battle.

The silence between us was deafening. Sophia stood there, eying me as grey ashes suspended into a limp line in the air and fell into the snow below with an audible sizzle.

For a split second, I thought that I saw the curtains in the bay window move. As I glanced in the direction of the house I could have sworn that I saw Betty's face just before the curtains shut. Sophia saw me taking notice and provided one final warning.

"I suggest that you get off my property before I call the police on you for trespassing." She took another drag before crushing the cigarette butt under her shoe.

Police, what was she talking about? In all the years I've known Sophia, why would she resort to that? "There's no need to go to extremes," I pleaded.

Sophia shrugged, "Dealer's choice." She crossed her thin arms over her chest.

What else was I to do? "Fine," I conceded, "I'll go. But at least tell her that I came by." I said louder than necessary. My volume gave Sophia a noticeable jolt.

Sophia rolled her eyes at me. "Fine."

I retreated down the steps, but before I left, I took one final look at the house. I desperately wanted to see Betty's face. The house was still. She wasn't coming out.

"And stop with all those flowers!" She hollered at me. "My house looks like a funeral parlour!" She coughed, nearly bringing up a lung.

"I could help make that a reality," I muttered under my breath.

"What was that?" The battle-axe called out as I sulked towards my truck.

I waved her off. "Nothing!" I yelled back.

I got into my truck and slammed the door. My heart sank. I couldn't help but worry that this was the end. All that effort, and my wife still wasn't willing to see me.

Now what? Suddenly, an idea came to mind. Why didn't I think of this sooner? What a fool I've been.

CHAPTER 18

Wyatt

Looking back, I recalled one time when I had almost proposed to Sabrina. Even then I didn't know for certain if asking Sabrina to marry me was the right thing to do, but my heart assured me that it was. And I would have carried through with my proposal, but my sister, Rachel, as usual, got in the way.

Rachel *always* gets in the way.

It was right after high school was finished, and Sabrina was preparing to leave for university at the end of the summer. I had been worried because I figured she'd go off to the city, find some guy in her dorm, one thing would lead to another, and I'd be the victim of the classic turkey dump.

What is a 'turkey dump' exactly? Well, it's when a high school couple goes off to university, usually to different schools. When they come home for Thanksgiving, one person often breaks up with the other, usually because they've found someone new, hence the term 'turkey dump'. I was concerned that she'd lose interest in me, and I'd be another victim headed for relationship slaughter.

I had fretted about what to do all summer leading up to her departure. I worked overtime at my dad's shop, and I even picked up some gigs mowing the lawns at Bob Collins' rental properties, all because I had a goal in mind: I was going to buy Sabrina a ring. I wasn't going to buy her some silly promise ring. No, I was looking at an engagement ring.

One Saturday as I was preparing to go to the city to make this major purchase, I was confronted by my annoying little sister. She demanded to know where I was going. Without even trying she annoyed the hell out of me. I tried to brush her off and replied sharply, "None of your business, punk."

"Does *Dad* know you're taking the car?" She emphasized.

"*Does Dad know you're taking the car?*" I mimicked her; the last thing I needed was for her to tattle on me.

She scowled at me, "Don't be a jerk."

"Takes one to know one," I muttered.

"Shut up, loser" was her comeback.

Then, she hesitated before saying anything else sarcastic. A sickly-sweet smile stretched from ear to ear, the kind that might melt dad's heart, but certainly not mine, and she asked coyly, "Can I come?"

She had her nerve! "No, I have things to do," I said sharply, putting the key into the ignition. If I slammed on the gas fast enough, I could possibly get away from this brat.

"Like what?" she enquired with false sweetness.

Try as I might to brush her off, she persisted in trying to accompany me on my shopping mission. She came around to the driver's side of the car, folded her arms across the frame of the open window and threatened, "If you go and don't take me, I'll tell Dad."

I knew that she meant business. She was just that ornery, so I relented because I felt that I had no other option in the moment.

On the way to the city, I tried to ignore her as best I could, but she howled along with the current top 40 on the radio sounding every bit like a wounded animal. I was so relieved when we reached the mall parking lot. I revelled in the opportunity to be rid of her for at least an hour while I did my shopping.

As we were about to go our own ways, she had the nerve, no, the audacity, to ask, "Can I have some money? Just 50 bucks? I don't get my allowance until the end of the week."

"No," I replied sharply. "I'm not made of money. I have to earn it."

She stomped her feet and started to wail like a child throwing a tantrum.

Reluctantly, I took out a few bills, slammed them into the palm of her hand, and told her to get lost for an hour.

I started with the budget jewelry store; I couldn't afford a high-end one. Most of the rings looked pretty, but when the salesperson took them out of the case, I nearly choked when I saw the price tag. How could people afford these? I guess that an adult with a regular paying job could but not a high school graduate working minimum wage. As the diamonds got smaller and smaller, so did the price tag. I felt sheepish for thinking about my budget compared to what would make my girlfriend happy.

"How about this one?" The salesperson brought out a white topaz. "It looks like a diamond, but it's a gemstone." She leaned over the counter, "No one will know the difference," she whispered.

The ring was nice. I liked how it sparkled. "How much?" The saleswoman flipped over the paper tag, and I nodded in agreement. "I'll take it." One day, I'd tell Sabrina the truth and get her a ring I could afford, once I had a well-paying job.

Before I had a chance to leave the store with my purchase in hand, I heard an annoying voice ask, "Whatcha doing?" while aggressively slurping back a cherry red slushy.

My hour reprieve was up. "Nothing," I grumbled.

"Doesn't look like 'nothing'." She leaned over the counter to get a better look. "Is that for your *girlfriend*?" she said in a sing-song voice. Rachel could be *so* irritating sometimes.

Trying my best not to inflame any hostility that could ruin my surprise, I admitted, "Yes, it's for Sabrina."

"Where's your shopping?" I asked quizzically.

She shrugged. "I didn't see anything I liked."

Automatically, I held out my hand for her to return the money that I had given to her.

"No." She turned away from me.

"Rachel-" I pressed, grabbing for her shoulder, but she shrugged out of my grasp.

"I'll tell Dad you took the car without asking." The snide little brat threatened again. She liked to push my buttons.

"Fine, but I'm not giving you a cent for the rest of the year," I replied.

"Whatever you say," she sang.

All the way home, Rachel kept asking me what it was that I had bought Sabrina, and whether it was for a special occasion. I tried to throw her off the scent, but she persisted.

"Wait," she paused, "you aren't going to ask her to marry you, are you?" Rachel was getting under my skin. "That would be like the worst idea *ever*."

Why would Rachel think that? She loved Sabrina.

I glanced at her, taking my eyes off the road for a moment.

"It would be such a mistake! You'll look desperate," she insisted.

"Excuse me!" I wasn't trying to tether Sabrina to me; we loved each other. "I'm not being desperate."

"I mean, what if you aren't meant to be together? What if she's meant to be with some hot chemistry nerd that she meets at university?"

"That's a crappy thing to say to me." Just because I wasn't heading off to school in the fall didn't make me dumb.

Rachel sighed. "It's just that she's got some growing to do, and it might not include you right now." When did she become so insightful? What if she was right? What if we weren't meant to be together? Some people come into your life for a reason, others for a season, and some stay a lifetime – or so I once read on a bumper sticker. Maybe Sabrina and I were just seasons.

"Don't you want Sabrina to have a chance to find her true self? You two are hardly adults." She looked out the window, deep in contemplation, "Maybe you have some growing to do first, too."

That felt profound for a fourteen-year-old. I wondered what television show or magazine she got that advice from. Certainly not from our dad. He didn't know that I was thinking of asking Sabrina! Seriously, where did she come up with this stuff? Suddenly, I was filled with dread, with a maxed-out credit card and a non-refundable ring. What had I done?

As soon as we got home, I headed straight for my room. Maybe Rachel was right, maybe I shouldn't ask Sabrina to marry me just yet.

I took the small white topaz ring and hid it at the bottom of my sock drawer. Maybe one day I'd gift it to Sabrina, or maybe not.

CHAPTER 19

Dana

Bryan. Could it have been him? I couldn't shake the thought from my mind even as I slept, and it still lingered long after I got into the shop this morning.

Nah! Definitely not Bryan. The more I thought about it, the less it made sense that Bryan was secretly in love with me. If Bryan liked me, he'd probably tell me – or he'd tell someone else in town, and then I'd hear it through the gossip mill. That made much more sense – or did it?

I flipped the OPEN sign, clicked on the miniature village lights, and turned the radio on low. How was it when you started thinking about someone that consumed all the functioning neurons in your brain, rendering you completely useless?

I didn't have a crush on Bryan, so why was I even thinking about him? Maybe Sabrina got into my head. She was always trying to get me to think from a different perspective – damn her!

I couldn't waste time thinking about this anymore. Today, I had poinsettia arrangements to prepare for the local nursing home, a wreath to make for the animal shelter's raffle, and boutonnieres for a

Christmas Eve wedding. People were counting on me, and my secret admirer, whoever he was, would just have to wait.

Bryan.

Stop it, brain! Focus!

In the middle of preparing my orders, the jingle of the store bells signalled the arrival of a customer. "I'll be right out!" I called from the walk-in fridge. I finished the last of the nursing home arrangements.

When I saw Mr. Snow, I smiled. Every week, for the last two months, he had come in to buy something special for his wife. Sometimes it was a houseplant, a stuffed animal or an arrangement. He was, by far, my best customer. He must love his wife so much to get her something thoughtful every week. Sometimes I felt guilty charging him full price, so I made a special discount just for him, except he didn't know it.

"Afternoon, Dana." His rosy cheeks popped into a meek smile. Over the last few weeks he seemed a bit more serious than his usual self. Sometimes the holidays bring out all sorts of emotions.

"What can I do for my favourite customer?" I leaned across the workbench, curious to hear what he'd like for the missus today.

"Well, maybe you can help me with something special." He said distractedly.

I watched as his fingers fumbled in the pocket of his faded camel-coloured jacket. For most of his life, Mr. Snow had worked in the local lumber yard, and his garment was tattered and beaten by the logs. It looked a little worse for wear today with a giant tear in the side. Maybe his wife hadn't had an opportunity to fix it just yet. She was a crafty lady, always knitting or sewing something special for others. He was a lucky man.

Eventually, he pulled from his pocket a small, faded picture of a woman and laid it on the counter.

I rolled up the sleeves of my plaid shirt. "Who is this?" I asked as I studied the image.

A gentle smile crept across his face, barely concealing his joy. Around here, blue-collar men didn't show many emotions.

"This is my wife," his eyes twinkled, "on our wedding day. We were married on Boxing Day 40 years ago next week."

I picked up the photograph for a closer look.

"Well," he added, "the church was free, and the decorations were still up from Christmas mass. No one questioned why there was a manger in our wedding photos," he laughed.

"Beautiful picture. I haven't seen your wife in ages," I remarked as I set the photo down.

Mr. Snow cleared his throat. "Neither have I," he mumbled under his breath.

"What's that again?" I asked, not sure that I had heard him correctly.

"Nothing," he replied and, seeming to change the topic, made a very moving request. "I was wondering if you'd help me restore the magic of the day by recreating her wedding bouquet." In her delicate hand, his wife held a collection of red and white roses, baby's breath, and holly all wrapped in a thick green ribbon.

His request brought tears to my eyes. Choking back emotion, I said, "I'd love to do this for you."

"Could you have it by Boxing Day so that I could give it to her for our anniversary?" He took the photo, folded it back into position, and placed it in the pocket over his heart.

I checked the stock and confirmed that I could make his Christmas wish come true. "You're a good egg, Dana. I've always thought so," he said. I wasn't sure what he meant by that. Maybe he was lost in the nostalgia of love or Christmas kindness, but I decided not to question it.

After he settled his bill, he added, "Oh, and before I forget, this was mixed in my mail yesterday. I think it's for you."

A rush of cold air sent chills up my spine as he exited the store leaving me holding another letter.

My fingertips fondled the glued crease of the envelope as I tried to decide whether or not I wanted to open it. My stomach lurched. Has Bryan written me another letter? Maybe I should confront him and put an end to this madness once and for all.

Unable to resist, I tore into the letter and read the contents aloud:

Dear Dana,

Do you ever wonder- what if? I wish I had taken a chance on love when we were young.

X

"What?" I shook my head. What does that mean?

This can't be Bryan. We don't have a history- what would there be to wonder about him? It had to be someone I had a missed connection with, and who didn't have some of those?

If I'm recalling the past correctly, there was only one person who might have wished he had taken a chance on me when we were younger, and it wasn't Bryan. No, it was someone much closer to me. Someone who was a commitment-phobe.

I don't know how my mind wandered there, but somehow it got there: Wyatt wasn't asking Sabrina to marry him. I knew how much it ate at her, not having his promise of forever. She wished and hoped, year after year, that her sweetheart would make an honest woman of her, only for nothing to happen.

The truth was that Sabrina wasn't Wyatt's first love. I was.

CHAPTER 20

Reggie

I didn't have any right to come to a place of worship, not on my own, at least. I was a sinner, just like everyone else in Mercer. Sure, Betty and I had gotten married in a church. We also had Maggie's Baptism at church, and we attended the occasional Easter Sunday mass. I wasn't a religious man, but it made my wife happy when we went. Secretly, I think she liked going back to the place where we tied the knot.

When I pulled open the heavy wooden doors, I immediately felt a sense of calm and detected the unmistakable aroma of incense. The scent took me back to our wedding day all those years ago, but I didn't have time for reminiscing. I had work to do.

Standing at the altar, adjusting arrangements of poinsettias, was the man I had come to see. I cleared my throat to get his attention. When he didn't turn around, I called out, "Hello, Father Erikson!" My voice boomed throughout the church, echoing through every nook and cranny so much so that I even startled myself.

Father Erikson jumped. I wonder if he thought he had seen the Holy Ghost. When he turned around, his eyebrows furrowed, and I could have sworn I heard him cuss under his breath. But surely, I was mistaken. A man of the cloth wouldn't swear, would he?

"What was that?" I called out, my orange toque gripped tightly between my fingers.

I watched Father Erikson compose himself. "Tabernacle," he said as he approached me adjusting his collar, "I need to clean it before mass. I was just reminding myself out loud," he coughed nervously, "Sometimes I talk out loud to myself."

"I think they make medication for that," I joked, trying to break the tension. When we were finally face to face, Father Erikson looked at me with a perplexed expression. We both knew that I didn't belong here.

"What can I help you with, Reggie?" He asked kindly, but hesitantly.

I gripped my toque tightly between my fingers, nervous about his response to my unusual request. "I want you to help me win Betty over," I said, my voice trembling.

I watched as a confused expression crossed his face. "Pardon?" Did the good man think I was joking?

I swallowed the lump of fear in my throat and repeated myself, trying to be a little more confident in my request. "I would like you to help me win my wife back, please."

"And why would I help you to do that?" he asked. I sensed that he was annoyed with me, after all, he'd been avoiding me since the little incident at my house.

I mustered a cheap response. "You're a man of the cloth, surely you'd help a member of your community?"

A surprised laugh escaped his pursed lips. "Help you? After what you did to the carolers?" He threw up his hands and laughed again.

"Perhaps I could have been a bit nicer to the children," I sheepishly admitted. "If only they had first asked if I wanted to hear any carols, I might not have been so surprised and taken aback," I offered defensively. Holiday spirit or not, those kids needed to work on their performance skills. The optics of me slamming the door in their faces, and them getting covered in a blanket of snow, spurred me to apologize deeply for what I had done. My begging hadn't worked on Betty or her sister, but perhaps it would work on him. Forgiveness was a big part of going to church, wasn't it?

Father Erikson didn't even bother to cover his face when he rolled his eyes at me. "They are just children, trying to spread a little holiday cheer." As he turned to walk away, shaking his head, he turned and said, "You could have apologized to them in the moment. You're only offering to do that now because you want something from me."

Ouch! He had a point. I should have done the right thing when I had the chance.

I dug deep; I was trying to be a better man. "Please, Father. I didn't mean to be so gruff when the kids came by." I wrung the toque harder in my hands. "I've been going through a lot." I looked down at my feet, ashamed. "That's not an excuse for what I did. I've been upset. Betty left me." I struggled to hold back tears. I stood there and let the emotions I'd been holding back trickle down my face.

"Reggie," his voice softened, "I didn't know. I thought you meant that you and Betty had a disagreement." He gestured for me to join him in one of the pews. "What happened?" he asked when we settled on the hard wooden seats.

"I took her for granted," I stammered. Then, I summarized recent events to him. I ran my fingers through my thinning hair. "I didn't appreciate her as I should have. I'm a fool."

Father Erikson nodded. I wasn't sure if he was empathizing with me or confirming that I was indeed a fool. "No one is perfect, Reggie. We all make mistakes." He extended his comforting hand to pat my back.

I felt more tears form and silently drip down my face, I batted them away before Father Erikson could see. I tasted the salt on my lips. I don't know if it was being in church or confessing that I was a mess, but this felt like a turning point to finally get things back on track.

"So, Reggie," he haltingly asked, "what do you need me to help you with?"

Finally, I felt that someone was on my side. There was hope for me yet!

"Father Erikson, I need you to help me pull off an epic surprise."

CHAPTER 21
WYATT

There was seldom time for a break at work, but when the opportunity presented itself today, I didn't hesitate to take it. I've had so much on my mind lately and I needed some peace and quiet so that I could sort things out. The holiday was hard enough as it was, but now thoughts of marriage were floating around in my head.

She loves me, she loves me not, I teased myself. As kids, I remember Rachel and I lying on the grass in the yard, sprawled out over a checkered picnic blanket. We'd pluck the petals off whatever flowers we found in the garden singing this little ditty. Dad would yell at us for ruining the plants, but we would be so engrossed in the silliness of childhood that we innocently ignored him.

I used to be able to make Rachel laugh so hard that she would cry just by blowing a handful of flower petals in her face. As much as she annoys me now, I can still hear her bubbling over with laughter all those years ago when times were better, when our relationship was better.

Even now, I have occasionally caught myself plucking the petals from the odd flower, wondering if someone thought of me like that. *Wyatt loves me, he loves me not* – but Dana didn't love me back, of that I was certain. That's what you get for having a crush on your childhood friend.

As time went on, it eventually became Sabrina and whatever affections we had for each other, which made all the difference; however, my world felt as if it were upside down. What was I to do? Was marriage in the cards for us? I threw on my toque and jacket and headed outside. I needed some fresh air to clear my head.

After insufficient time alone, my silent retreat was broken when Fletcher barrelled through the back door. "Hey, man. The phone's ringing off the hook." He palmed his face. "I need some help." He ushered me back inside.

"Coming," I huffed, and headed back in. He was right, every red button on the phone was lit up. I probably went through 10 slips of paper writing down orders and appointments. Dad would be pleased with the amount of business, but at the same time he wanted to close shop for a bit over the holiday, said he needed to get away. That wasn't like him; he was usually a workaholic. I wondered what was up with him.

After the commotion died down, and we were finishing up for the day, Reggie came into the shop. "Wyatt! I need to talk to you about my order. I need to make a change in it." Reggie panted as he rushed inside.

"What's wrong?" I asked. This isn't the first time Reggie has come in to change an order for parts he wanted to restore the car he'd been working on, but something was amiss from the way he was almost hyperventilating.

He cast his eyes towards the floor. "I think I've gone a bit over budget." He threw his gloves down on the counter. "I want to change some items and cancel a few things I can do without." He grumbled.

Reggie had been working on his car for years. He meticulously selected every item, even expensive custom orders from out of the country. Considering how hard he'd been working on that car it was hard to believe that he would settle for anything but original pieces for it, the price be damned. Nevertheless, the customer is always right. Besides, I knew that he had been going through a tough time and probably needed the money for something else.

As Reggie and I reviewed his original order, I couldn't help but notice that he seemed off, like he was having a hard time concentrating. I recalled the brief conversation we had earlier at *Bean There, Done That* and I worried about him. He hadn't been himself lately, and now it made sense, considering what he said about Betty.

On the spur of the moment, I decided to reach out to Reggie, and I said, "Before you go, I was wondering if you wanted to join us at *Lucky's Pub* for trivia tomorrow night?" Perhaps I should've asked the girls if it was okay to invite him, but I'm sure they wouldn't mind just this once.

"That's very kind of you," he replied. Initially, I thought that he was going to reject my offer, but then he said, "I'd love to." His eyes were bright with joy. There could be no question that, without Betty around, Reggie wanted to fill the emptiness he was feeling with any distraction.

I wrote my number on a piece of paper and handed it to him. Sabrina was always complaining that my handwriting looked like chicken scratch, but it seemed legible to me.

Reggie's face brightened, filled with confidence. "Thanks, Wyatt. I'll see you then."

It was a nice feeling to help him out during the holidays.

Not long after Reggie left, Fletcher and I closed the shop for the night. I declined his offer for a smoke, but the beer that he suggested might just hit the spot after such a rough day at work. Having a drink with the boys at the pub, just to relax, was becoming a habit, one that did not sit well with Sabrina. Was I subconsciously avoiding spending time with her? I didn't think so. I had real feelings for Sabrina, ones that I needed to act on. Reluctantly, I declined the offer of drinks making the lame excuse that I really should spend more time with my family, especially my little sister at home.

Fletcher's smile grew. "Rachel is home?" He bit his lip as he zipped up his leather jacket.

"Don't get any ideas. She's *my sister*." Throwing Rachel to Bryan was one thing, but I didn't want Fletcher sinking his fangs into my family.

Fletcher put out his cigarette and kicked himself off against the wall that he had been leaning against. We headed towards our vehicles.

"I'm just teasing you. See you later, Wyatt," Fletcher called out from across the parking lot. He hopped into his jeep, revved the engine and took off. I'm sure he wouldn't have any trouble finding a lady at the pub tonight. Surely, eventually, Fletcher would want to find a partner, wouldn't he?

I got into my car, but I couldn't stop thinking about Reggie. The poor guy has been home alone for the last couple of months, pining after his wife. What was the point of marriage if four decades of love came crumbling down just like that? His predicament didn't do anything to help me resolve my dilemma about whether to propose to Sabrina or not.

CHAPTER 22

Dana

Every Thursday night, without fail, Sabrina, Wyatt and I headed down to the local pub to test our wits. Going out was my test to see if I could re-enter society. We usually booked a table, played trivia and laughed at the dimwits who frequented the only pub in town, *Lucky's Pub*. In some ways, we weren't much better. I sat, for what felt like an eternity, mulling over the new facts I was sure I had found out about my admirer.

For the few hours between reading the second letter and meeting with Sabrina, my brain was in overdrive. How could I continue the hunt for my secret admirer when the obvious answer was right in front of me?

Over the last decade or so, I had watched Sabrina and Wyatt's relationship grow from friends to lovers with a brief interlude of foes. It was obvious to everyone that they were perfect for each other. Sabrina was an independent person who loved camping and teaching paddle boarding at the canoe club. Wyatt didn't mind that she did her own thing, and she didn't mind that he spent most of his time working for his dad at the shop, until recently.

There was always something peculiar about Wyatt. Don't get me wrong, he has been one of my best friends since elementary school, but he never seemed to take the leap to marriage with Sabrina, and no one could figure out why.

I couldn't help but think back to junior high school, as that's when things turned between us.

I recalled that our moms were friends before Wyatt's mom took off. They would often schedule playdates for us so they could enjoy their coffees and gossip about all the things they'd heard around town.

Things took a romantic turn for him and me in class one day when I brought a cartoon mouse doll in for 'show and tell.' No one seemed enthusiastic about my hand-me-down, but when we were alone, Wyatt told me how cool he thought the doll was. For a split second, I felt as if he liked me for me, and the next thing I knew, I threw the doll over my head, wrapped my arms around Wyatt and kissed him. The consequence was that I had to sit in front of Principal King's office until I learned my lesson. The lesson included missing out on Mrs. McLachlan's chicks hatching in our classroom incubator.

That kiss between Wyatt and me sparked a childhood connection of a faux wedding in the playground, biking on the trails that wove the tapestry of our small town together and watching R-rated horror movies on the internet. I got away with a lot when I was a kid.

Most of our childhood was spent together. When Wyatt's mom left his dad, Wyatt would spend a lot of dinners with us, so he didn't have to be at home alone with Rachel and his dad. I couldn't imagine the heartache he experienced.

Looking back, we went through a lot. We were there for each other for the good times and the bad. He was like a brother to me. We were inseparable until the sands of time told us that we had to pair up or part ways. Inevitably, little boys become wannabe young men, and suddenly, someone you once had sleepovers with becomes the object of your affection.

The script was flipped during lunchtime in 8th grade. Wyatt and I, as usual, sat at our lone table in the cafeteria, talking about the latest video game that was coming out for the holidays. My brothers had left their gaming system at home when they moved away to college, and I had the luxury of using it, even though I had to borrow games from Wyatt.

Innocently enough, I had gone on and on about beating the last level of the fad game of the moment. Wyatt had listened to me drone on as I became lost in the story of the epic battle of the pixilated creature. I failed to notice, as I told my grand story, that Wyatt had reached his hand across the table towards me. I was brought back to reality when I felt the soft touch of his clammy fingers.

Wyatt was trying to hold my hand. Why the hell would he do that?

I looked up at him as his chapped lips were trying to suck soda through a warped straw. His large, brown eyes met mine, hopeful. Who was this guy? Was he trying to make a move on me? I've seen him eat boogers and cut worms in half to see if they would wiggle away. This guy could *not* be serious.

I shifted my gaze downward to witness this foreign form of affection, and before I could say anything, he tore his hand away from mine. It might have been the look of disgust and horror on my face because after that, he didn't speak to me for an entire week.

I tried so hard to talk to him. I sent text messages to him, rode my bike past his house, I even called his landline. He wouldn't sit with me on the bus ride home. He'd get off the bus a few stops earlier so he didn't have to see me. I tried to pass notes to him in class, but he ignored my efforts. The teacher caught on and confiscated whatever olive branch I was extending at that moment. When, eventually, I succeeded in securing a second with him, he shrugged off the interaction of affection like it was no big deal.

Should I have reciprocated when he reached for me?

The long answer was *no*.

While Wyatt was ignoring me, I met a new student named Sabrina in gym class. Since we were from different small towns, our paths didn't cross until junior high. We laughed and bonded over our shared nemesis, the popular girls, and learned that we had similar interests in rock bands. I finally had a friend whose raging hormones didn't interfere with mine.

I made one last attempt to reconcile with Wyatt before I decided to give up. I had been eating lunch with Sabrina one day, and Wyatt walked by. He was on his own, carrying his lunch tray of poutine. He glanced at me and then quickly averted his gaze. I wish he'd pretend that his failed attempt at romance hadn't happened because it would have been best for both of us to forget.

"Hey, Wy!" I called after him. I had seen him swing his leg over a bench, ready to eat alone. "Come join us." Wyatt nervously looked around, and when he saw that I wasn't alone, he took the bait and came over. Finally! Maybe having a buffer helped him feel comfortable in my company.

"Hey," he glanced briefly at me, but continued to avoid making eye contact. I couldn't help but feel like a stranger to my best friend, of all people. Would entering our teens erase the years of friendship between us?

I let out an exasperated sigh, "This is Sabrina." I gestured to my new friend. "And this is my best friend, Wyatt," I said to her. Wyatt looked up awkwardly at her. Instead of the cold glance I got, I swore I saw cartoon hearts pop up in his eyes. I couldn't help but feel a pang of jealousy. My best friend was slipping away. Maybe I didn't want him, but that didn't mean I was ready for him to fall for someone else.

Teenage feelings can be *so* complicated.

"Hey," Sabrina conjured, and with that, her crooked smile opened as wide as physically possible, revealing the green and blue elastics on her braces. Years later, she'd have one of the most beautiful smiles I'd ever seen.

"Hey," he returned the greeting. I couldn't help but cringe over their awkward exchange as I reflected in the moment on the beginning of their budding romance.

And that was the start of Wyatt and Sabrina. It would take a couple of years for them to officially start dating, but they would be flexible to grow together.

I couldn't help but think back to junior high: what if I had given Wyatt a chance? Would we have become a couple?

CHAPTER 23

Reggie

After several long talks with Father Erikson, Wyatt, and Maggie, I felt that I had a better plan in place.

I didn't know how much longer I could take coming home to any empty house. Bruce is the only constant in my life lately. He's been good company, but he doesn't replace Betty.

On the advice of Father Erikson, I decided to put up a small Christmas tree. Lucky for me, they were sharply discounted at the tree lot now that Christmas was just around the corner. Father Erikson thought that by putting up a tree I would remember the special moments I used to share with Betty. He suggested I could come to Sunday mass, and if I felt up to it, confession. The last thing I needed was to repent for my sins; I'd been doing enough of that in private. But, then again, if it helped, I guessed I'd do it.

I'd do anything for Betty.

When the last ornament was up, I took a step back and admired my handiwork. My decorating skills paled in comparison to Betty's, but it would do. I'd leave the rest of the Christmas decorations for tomorrow. My back was beginning to bother me. I needed a rest before I headed out to *Lucky's Pub* and joined Wyatt and his friends in a game of trivia.

So, I shuffled into the kitchen to get a beer. I cracked the cap off and headed into the living room. I dimmed the lights, taking in the festive view.

My shoulders sagged as I slumped into my recliner. I tried to relax, but I couldn't get comfortable. As I twisted about in the chair I came face to face with a small, white ornament. It had the intricate etching of a snowflake that had faded from years of use. I couldn't help but hold it, inspecting it. The memory slowly returned to me. This was the ornament that Betty and I bought on our wedding day, the happiest day of my life.

It didn't take much effort to recall that day. Neither of us had much money; Betty and I had come from humble backgrounds. My job at the yard barely covered the cost of her wedding band. I saved up to buy that at a pawn shop. I wanted to give her something special, but I couldn't afford a proper engagement ring. I had proposed to her with a twist tie and promised her that one day I'd buy her a real diamond, but I never did. She laughed at me and said that she didn't need anything else if she had me.

I recalled approaching Father George at our church in the past. Initially, he tried to convince us to wait until we were a little older. He said that we both had some growing up to do, and that in a couple of more years we would be ready for a nice church wedding. We reassured him that we were in love and ready for a lifetime commitment to each other. After some swaying, he finally agreed to marry us. Father George offered us the church on Boxing Day. He said that it would be romantic with the Christmas decorations still up, and it wouldn't cost us any money. Betty and I were sold on the idea.

On the day of the wedding, Betty wore her mother's ivory lace wedding dress. Her mother had saved it for her. There had been a little kerfuffle with Sophia, but their mother assured her that both daughters could wear the dress for their special days, if they wanted to.

Before the ceremony started, there was a big commotion. My bride was frantically throwing her arms in the air, and tears were flowing down her perfectly painted face. She and Sophia had argued. The fight escalated and, as a result, her entire family left, ruining Betty's special day. Our small guest list suddenly became smaller. Betty never told me what had been said, but I knew that she was devastated when her family didn't witness our marriage and celebrate our matrimony.

My parents, who loved Betty, sat in the front row. They were delighted that I had found such a lovely young lady to share my life with, and they immediately welcomed her into our family. They also wed right out of high school, so they never questioned our decision. Still, I felt a pang of sadness for my bride. I vowed to make her happy for the rest of my life, whatever the cost.

When the tears were dried, and what few guests in attendance had taken their places, ancient Mrs. Myers sat down at the organ. She cracked her knuckles, causing me, my parents, and Father George to wince. The Wedding March filled every hollow space of the church, the doors opened, and my blushing bride walked down the aisle on my father's arm. He had stepped in to fill her father's shoes without even being asked.

The closer they got to the altar where I waited with Father George, the more I realized that Betty and I were destined to be. Then, when they reached the front of the church, my father lifted her veil and gently kissed her on her cheek. I heard him whisper to her, "Welcome to the family, love," as he guided her hand toward mine.

I sure do miss my folks. They were good people. Whenever I glance at their photo on our mantelpiece, I nod my head towards them, thanking them for everything they've given me in life.

Sometimes I wonder where I went wrong. How did I stray from the man my parents raised? I shook my head, refocusing my attention on the white ornament and being transported back to our wedding day.

When the vows were said, and the last picture was snapped, Betty and I ran outside, trying to outrun the stream of rice being thrown at us by Father George, Mrs. Myers and my parents. I yanked open the door of my car, helped my bride inside, and we took off for Niagara Falls, Canada's then-honeymoon capital.

I paused, chuckling to myself. That was a wonderful day, even if it didn't turn out quite as planned. Sometimes life is funny like that, but that doesn't mean that you give up.

CHAPTER 24
Wyatt

There have been more nights than I'd like to admit that I have had nightmares about that day. No, I don't mean when I backed away from proposing to Sabrina, although I do kick myself occasionally over that decision.

No, another memory haunted me – my mom.

Try as I might to forget, I remember so vividly the day she left our family.

It was a Thursday, right before the Christmas holiday. It was a normal day: our mom packed our lunches – leftover pizza for me, and a grilled cheese sandwich for Rachel. Our metal lunch boxes were filled to the brim with granola bars, fruit snacks and a bag of chips. Our lunches were the envy of all the kids in our classes.

Mom would drive us to school in her old maroon Buick. Dad would wash and shine that car every weekend, even in the winter, until it sparkled. Mom used to joke that she was our chauffeur, and she'd drive us wherever we pleased. Sometimes we'd beg for her to take us to the convenience store for a slushy after school. Most Fridays, we'd get our wish. She'd turn the radio up loud and sing along with the latest hits. She was so much fun to be around; it was as if she were a kid herself.

When I think back, nothing abnormal stood out about our last day together. When we parked in front of the school, Mom told us to wait a minute before we got out. She took a long look at us, smiled, and seemed to study our faces. As always, she told us that she loved us, but maybe, just maybe, when I think back about that day, that 'I love you' hit different. Little did I know that, when I shut the car door, she was leaving us for good.

At the end of the school day, our mom was usually the first in line to collect her offspring, but not that particular day. That day, Rachel and I were left standing in the freezing cold. I was consumed with worry. My heart was beating against my ribcage as if trying to escape.

Mrs. Hartman, the school secretary, came out to collect us. Rachel and I sat in the front lobby of the school, sipping hot chocolate she had made us while we waited. I had wondered what was going on. I could see Mrs. Hartman and Principal King huddled together, having a secret conversation. Occasionally, they'd glance over at us with sad looks in their eyes.

By the time Dad arrived at the school, it was dark outside. He rushed through the front doors, apologizing profusely to Principal King who had stayed behind to watch us. I could have sworn that he had been crying; his eyes were red. He rushed over and wrapped his arms around us. He apologized and promised us that we'd have a special meal when we got home. Rachel looked up at him, doe-eyed and clueless – she had no idea what was going on. She was just happy that our dad was here and that she'd get to go home and play with her dolls. I, however, knew something wasn't right.

What happened to our mom?

Dinner that night was extra cheesy macaroni with a soft drink, something usually reserved for the weekend because mom said that neither of those were healthy food choices. Dad's exceptions were just another clue to me that something was amiss in our household.

Rachel asked, innocent of the goings on, "When's mommy coming home?"

Dad just smiled weakly and said, "Soon, I hope."

Meanwhile, I pushed the food around my plate. I had lost my appetite. "Where did she go?" I had to ask, and I think that was a fair question.

Dad ignored me and stared down at his half eaten plate of food. So, I waited a few minutes and asked again.

He slammed his cutlery on the table and in a raised voice said, "Damn it, Wyatt. I don't know!"

Tears welled in my eyes. Boys weren't supposed to cry, so I launched my chair back from the table, with a screech across the hardwood floor, and ran to my room. Dad did his best to apologize, but I wasn't about to come back to the table. I slammed my bedroom door shut and threw myself onto my bed. I cried until the tears were all gone.

A couple of times in the evening, Dad came to my room to check on me. I refused to open the door for him when he knocked.

When I was convinced that everyone was asleep, I got up and tried to quietly open the zipper on my backpack. I reached inside and pulled out a picture I had painted in art class – one of my family standing in front of a colourful Christmas tree, surrounded by presents. I took one final look at it and tore it in two.

There was no more happy family. My mom was gone, and she wasn't coming back anytime soon, if ever.

***

On Christmas Day, Dana's parents, Stu and Eva, invited us over to open our gifts. Dana didn't know what had happened yet, but her parents were aware of what had occurred in the Greene household and were commiserating in hushed whispers with my dad.

"I can't believe that Carol up and left," Dad said as he cradled his drink. I inched closer to hear what the adults were saying. They stood in a circle in the dining room, away from us kids playing nearby with the Christmas gifts.

"Do you think she'll come back, Lou?" Stu asked as perplexed as everyone else.

"I don't know, Stu," he said; he sounded defeated, "for the kids' sake, I hope she does." My dad took a moment to scan the room. I leaned back from my perch on the other side of the doorway and ducked before he could see me.

Eva placed a hand on Dad's forearm. "Do you know why she left?" she looked at him with sympathetic eyes. Why would a mother leave her family?

Dad sighed, "We fought." he took two long swigs of eggnog. "And we *never* fight." The voices were scrambled momentarily as a board game escalated in the living room.

"Kids! What did I tell you? Be careful!" Eva yelled, aware of the commotion in the next room. "Be careful of that crystal vase! That was your grandmother's vase, Dana!" She shouted at my bestie.

"Sorry, Mom! We'll be more careful," Dana reassured her from the other room.

When I resumed my eavesdropping post, I was joined by my sister. She was too young to get involved in any emotional warfare that my mother had initiated. As her big brother, I would take on the responsibility of protecting her innocence.

The adults were very guarded in their conversation and Rachel was persistently wanting to know what I was doing hovering in the doorway. I was missing a crucial part of the conversation, and I didn't want her to give me away.

Momentarily, I lost my cool and angrily whispered at her to "buzz off." Then, I felt guilty. Rachel needed to be sheltered from whatever speculation there was about our mom's disappearance. She didn't need me to make matters worse. Fortunately, she was not offended by my outburst and returned to the living room to play with the others.

I managed to hear Stu say, "I hope Carol comes back, for everyone's sake."

"She may, or she may not. Who knows." My dad's eyes were bloodshot and glossy.

"Let's have some hope," Eva tried to reassure him. "Fights happen. We've all been there."

Dad shook his head, "Not like this one; this one was really bad," his voice quivered. "And at the holidays, too. How could she leave without saying anything?"

"We're here for you and the kids," Stu reassured him, giving my dad a side embrace.

"I don't know if I'll ever trust another woman again." Dad sighed as he polished off his drink, emptying his cup and his heart.

To be honest, I felt the same way as my dad did in that moment. What was the point of falling in love if someone might obliterate your heart?

CHAPTER 25
Dana

Fast forward to now. I sat in *Lucky's Pub*, under the twinkling white Christmas lights, reminiscing about my past.

"They don't have your favourite IPA, so I got you a lager instead," Sabrina said as she plunked my drink down. Foam sloshed over the edge of the pint glass, wetting the paper coaster beneath it. "Earth to Dana, do you copy?" Sabrina flashed her hand in front of my eyes. "Are the lights giving you a seizure?" She stirred the contents of her glass and pressed the rim close to her lips. "If so, you're out of luck. The closest hospital is a half hour away." She took a sip of her vodka soda.

I took a deep breath and steadied myself and tried to decide what to say. I wanted to tell Sabrina the truth: I believed that the reason her boyfriend wasn't proposing to her was because of me.

Before I could say anything, one of the legs of the wooden chair screeched across the floor, drowning out the latest melancholic rendition of a classic Christmas song. "Did I miss anything?" the overly enthusiastic voice asked. He took a swig from his beer bottle and set it down on the table.

"The game hasn't started yet. You haven't missed a thing, Wyatt." Sabrina reassured him. "You're right on time."

CHAPTER 26

Reggie

When I got up the next morning, I decided to put out the rest of the Christmas decorations. My mood had lifted, if only slightly. Maybe Father Erikson was onto something after all. I used to love Christmas, and this year didn't need to be an exception.

I started with my morning routine of attempting to make coffee and feeding the damn cat. In the living room I found the flimsy old cardboard box with the rest of the decorations and dug inside. One of the ornaments had fallen out of the shoebox we usually kept them in. I took the tissue paper off to see which one hadn't made it to the tree yet. Lo and behold, it was the most special one of all: the ornament we bought on our honeymoon.

We had a wonderful time in Niagara Falls. From the moment we were engaged, Betty talked nonstop about that place, having been mesmerized by some old movies with the thundering waterfalls in the background. She brought home every library book or brochure she could find, outlining some of the things she wanted to see or do if she ever made it there.

I remember how excited Betty was when I told her we were heading there right after the wedding, so long as the roads were clear. The last thing I needed to do was get us stranded in a snowstorm. Luckily, Mother Nature was on our side for the journey south.

"How much further is it?" She'd ask every so often, like an excited child. Occasionally, we had to pull over at a gas station so I could unfold the map because I was in unfamiliar territory and the weather was not cooperating. I'd tell Betty a little white lie about the distance just to set her at ease, but I wasn't exactly sure how much farther it was going to be.

Even though the driving time dragged on, Betty didn't seem to mind. I remember looking down from time to time to see her fingers laced between mine as we headed to our romantic destination.

When we finally arrived, Betty clapped her hands excitedly as I rounded the car to open her door. She jumped out and fell into my arms. She must not have been aware that it was already morning by the time we finally arrived. The roads had been clear for the most part, but I drove carefully wherever it was icy and the drive had seemed endless to me.

The door chimed as we excitedly burst through into the lobby. The clerk jolted awake as if he had been hit by a bolt of lightning. "Welcome to the Misty Motel. How can I help you?" The clerk smiled at us with bloodshot eyes. A crease had stretched across his face from the makeshift pillow on his desk.

Betty and I smiled at each other. "Reservations for Mr. and Mrs. Snow," I beamed at my wife as I said her new surname for the first time. "We're on our honeymoon." I raised my eyebrows and wiggled them at my bride.

"Congratulations," the clerk said, enthusiastically extending his well wishes. "But you were supposed to arrive last night, according to our logbook."

"Yes," I cleared my throat. "The weather...." I trailed off as the clerk nodded, signalling that he understood our dilemma. "I'm happy to pay for last night," I reassured him.

The clerk raised his hand in protest. "No, these things do happen." In a flash, his starched red blazer spun around in a circle. He reached up to a board and then said, "The Honeymoon Suite," as he handed us our key.

Betty's eyes grew wide, and her smile stretched across her face. "Really?" she said, overwhelmed. We hadn't booked that room because it was considerably more money than we had for a few nights' stay.

Sensing my hesitation, he said, "It's on the house." He winked as he offered to take our bags to our room. How could I resist? Betty was thrilled at this pleasant surprise.

Once in the room, and we were alone, Betty spun around in circles. "Can you believe this, Reggie? The Honeymoon Suite!" She explored every nook and cranny: the oversized bed with a fluffy white duvet, the balcony with a slight view of the falls and last, but not least, a red heart-shaped bathtub. "Oh, Reggie! This is amazing!"

I smiled, proud that the few short hours of married life brought so much joy to her, particularly considering the wedding mishap with her family. "And look, we even have a bottle of sparkling wine!" I held up the bottle and two glass flutes.

"Maybe we can save that for this evening," she wrapped me in a loving embrace. I rubbed her bare arms, still cold from the winter temperature.

"Shall I warm you up, Mrs. Snow?" I cooed in her ear.

"Why, yes, Mr. Snow." She kissed me on the lips. I think I could get used to having a wife.

"I need to freshen up after that long drive, then I will meet you in pillow paradise." I gestured towards the bed then made my way into the bathroom and showered.

When I was towelled off and refreshed, I gently opened the door and re-entered the bedroom. "Mrs. Snow…" I stopped when I saw that my wife was sound asleep under the blankets. I sat on the bed beside her and stroked her hair. "Rest up, my sweet. There's plenty of time for us to enjoy each other's company." With that, I turned the lights off, curled up with my new wife, and fell asleep, too.

CHAPTER 27

Wyatt

It was almost midnight by the time I got home from *Lucky's Pub*. Sabrina decided to stay over with Dana and brainstorm about who knows what. I didn't argue, I was happy to have the bed to myself tonight.

From the driveway where I parked the car, I could see that the living room light was still on, and I realized that Rachel was likely still awake. I didn't have the patience to talk to her now. She had been grilling me about my future, particularly my marital status. What did she care? She wasn't my mother! I didn't even have one of those.

I felt a vibration in my pocket; maybe it was Sabrina, but no, when I looked, I saw that it was Reggie calling. I wondered what was up.

"Hello?" I asked cautiously, as if the phone were going to explode.

"Wyatt!" He said a little too cheerfully. "I didn't wake you, did I?"

"Not at all. I just got home." An awkward pause or two skipped between us. "Is everything alright?" I asked, concerned. Most people text these days, calling wasn't the norm anymore. But, then again, Reggie was an older gentleman.

"Yes, oh yes. I-" he chuckled, as if unsure whether to continue, "I wanted to thank you for inviting me tonight."

I felt my face blush.

"It's just that I've become used to sitting alone at home, and you made my night. I hope I wasn't too much of a bother," Reggie trailed off.

I shook my head 'no' but then foolishly realized that he couldn't see me. "Not at all, Reggie, we were glad you came." The truth was that Sabrina and Dana were somewhat annoyed with Reggie joining us. We usually came in first place but tonight we had lost; however, I told him that we did well because of him and then laughed to lighten the mood.

"That's a relief. At first, I was worried about Dana. She seemed a little irked with me." Reggie said reluctantly.

"Oh, don't worry about her, Reggie, she's got a lot on her mind lately." That was an understatement. I couldn't help but notice how distracted she had been all night.

"What's going on? Anything I can do to help?" Concern flooded his voice.

I wasn't sure if I should give him the full details. Dana didn't like everyone knowing her business after what happened, but I'm sure a small tidbit wouldn't hurt. "She's been receiving letters from a 'secret admirer' and she's trying to figure out who it is." I air quoted, "I don't think she needs to worry too much about him. He's harmless."

"Oh, you know who's sending her the letters?" Reggie asked with curiosity.

"Not for certain, but I've got a hunch." I stifled a yawn. "Anyway, don't worry too much about her. I've known her most of my life and she can be a handful sometimes." We both laughed, seemingly in agreement.

"Well, thanks again." And just as I thought, Reggie was about to wish me a goodnight, he said, "Oh, and just one other thing. I was wondering, after our little talk, whether you bought Sabrina something *special* for this Christmas?" He emphasized.

Now, it seemed as if I had to contend with both my sister and Reggie meddling in my life.

CHAPTER 28

Dana

In a further attempt at solving my mystery, I decided to go rogue. I didn't want to upset Sabrina with my suspicion that Wyatt was withholding a proposal because he still held a torch for me. I needed to extinguish this flame, and fast. Wyatt belonged with Sabrina.

Before work, I decided to head over to *Lou's Auto Body Shop*. The snow had started to blow hard this morning, making my trek rather wicked. When I arrived, the door was locked, but Wyatt's vehicle was parked outside. It looked like he was alone inside, so I rattled the door to summon my crush, who was about to be crushed.

"Hold your horses!" Wyatt called out. He brushed the glossy brown hair from his eyes. He'd been working so much lately that he hadn't had it cut. To be honest, I thought that long hair looked good on him. Come to think of it, his overalls hugged him in all the right places, too.

I had to warn myself to stop admiring my best friend's boyfriend!

"We need to talk." I slammed the letters into his oil-stained hand. He looked down, confused.

"Okay," he drawled. He sat down and thumbed through the letters. "So, did you figure out who wrote these?"

I stared at him, dumbfounded.

"You." I huffed. "Stop playing games, Wyatt. This is serious!" I stood up, throwing my arms above my head. "You can't be in love with me when you're in love with my best friend!"

He stared at me, his mouth hanging open in shock. He was obviously dumbstruck by my accusation.

It was then that I realized, sheepishly, Wyatt was not my secret crush.

"Let me get this straight, you think I'm in love with you?" he asked. He stared at me as if I had two heads.

My face warmed with embarrassment. "I guess that it does sound a bit off, doesn't it?" I had to admit. My face felt like it was engulfed in flames.

"Ya think?" He stood up and walked over to the truck he was working on. I'd try to leave this conversation, too, if I were in his shoes.

"Dana, we've been friends, no, family, for nearly our entire lives. I love you like a sister, but it ends there." He fiddled with some tools at his workstation.

I thought back to the cafeteria in junior high, I felt that I needed to set the record straight.

"What about that time in middle school when you tried to hold my hand at lunch?"

He stopped whatever he was doing and searched his memories. "What are you talking about?" He furrowed his eyebrows, as if deep in thought, and, at the same time, continued to try to work on the truck.

I walked around the vehicle to face him. "You tried to hold my hand!" I placed my hands on my hips and tapped my foot, trying to shake out some of my anxiety.

Wyatt shut his eyes in frustration. "I think you've got this wrong. You were so nervous talking to me, going on and on about some silly game. I only tried to hold your hand *down* because you were going to hit me in the face with your flailing spaghetti limbs. And when you saw my hand on yours, I could see joy in your face. I was afraid that you were in love with *me*."

"That's not how it went!" I contended.

"Yes, it was. You were obsessed with me. You wouldn't stop calling my house or texting me. When you came by, I begged my dad to tell you I wasn't home."

"How dare you flip this script!" I said with a raised voice.

"It's true! You were *so* in love with me. I couldn't believe what happened." He smirked. "You changed and became boy crazy." He shook his head.

"Wyatt, you fib. This is *not* how it went down." The case I had built for him, being in love with me, was totally and utterly shattered. How could I have been so wrong?

"Whatever you say, Dana. Whatever you say." He finished what he was doing and filled out an invoice for the repair work.

"Okay, so if it isn't you who is in love with me, then why haven't you asked Sabrina to marry you yet?" I tried to pivot the conversation away from my embarrassment. I wanted to know why he hadn't made an honest woman of my best friend.

Wyatt turned on his heels to face me, his work boots squeaking on the floor. "Why is everyone so obsessed with marriage?" He paced the shop like a caged bachelor. "It's not like *you* want to get married."

Realizing his faux pas, he murmured, "Sorry." Momentarily, the silence was deafening.

"Marriage isn't in the cards for everyone, jerk." My face reddened, both with humiliation over being wrong about Wyatt and what I had done.

He tucked a rag into his back pocket. "I said I was sorry!" he pleaded.

"Okay, well, figure it out. You don't want Sabrina to leave you." I folded my arms across my chest. Wyatt could do worse than to end up with Sabrina.

Panic struck his face. "Does she want to leave me?" His eyes grew wide like saucers.

"That's not-" he cut me off before I could finish.

"What did she say?" his voice quivered.

"I didn't say she was leaving you. I meant that you don't want her to find someone else." Truthfully, I could never imagine Sabrina leaving Wyatt, unless, of course, he did something heinous.

"But she's not leaving me? Is she?"

"No," I tried to reassure him. The last thing I wanted to do was to inadvertently break them up!

"Thank God," he whispered, putting a hand over his panicked heart.

"Either way, figure your life out. She's a catch," I told him. I knew that Sabrina and Wyatt had a better chance of getting married than I ever would.

"I know she's a catch," he paused to reflect, "but what if I'm not?"

"What's that supposed to mean?" I guess we all have insecurities, even men.

"Nothing." He clammed up.

"Wyatt, come on. What's wrong?" I searched his eyes for an answer.

"Maybe I'm not the marrying kind." He hung his head low. "I don't want to turn out like my parents."

For the next hour, before opening, Wyatt and I rehashed his mom's leaving him and his family, and the insecurities that her decision had imprinted on his life. He never found out why she left; it was a sore spot in their family history. A family home wasn't broken until someone took away the foundation.

CHAPTER 29

Reggie

Betty and I had a whirlwind few days on our honeymoon. We did everything that you can possibly do in Niagara Falls: we took a boat ride under the falls, strolled along the walkway by the waterfront, and played all the carnival-like games on Clifton Hill. We snapped endless pictures for a lifetime of memories all the while soaking in this natural wonder of the world. And, what impressed me most, what I will always truly appreciate, was Betty's beautiful smile.

We stopped in one of the many gift shops just before leaving to return to Mercer; Betty had a craving for saltwater taffy. "Look at this," she said as she spun a showcase around. She was admiring a collection of Christmas ornaments that were on display. Blue and white painted waterfalls decorating round ceramic ornaments, some engraved with 'Honeymoon Capitol', hung with red ribbons. But Betty gravitated towards one of the more, shall I say, tacky ornaments. The words 'Niagara Falls' were painted like bright neon lights on a brittle white sphere. The thing looked horrendous, but the smile on her face was priceless.

"You want that one?" I asked hoping she wasn't choosing an inexpensive souvenir just because of me. Surely, she'd prefer something more. I wouldn't mind spending a bit of extra cash if she wanted a fancy one.

"Yes. It's different," she said, and her eyes sparkled. I realize now that Betty was creating a memory of our time away as husband and wife.

"Then we'll take it." I paid for it at the register, and we headed back home. Home, at that time, was my parents' basement. We couldn't afford a down payment for a house yet, so they let us live there for next to nothing until we could move out.

The ride up north was eventless; we still hadn't discussed why her family hadn't come to the wedding; however, when we returned home, that talk was inevitable. Sophia's car was parked in my parents' driveway.

"She's here," Betty groaned. "Hasn't she done enough?"

I wished I knew exactly what had transpired. I felt sorry for Betty. Couldn't we all just get along? "What do you want to do?" I squeezed my wife's hand. "I'll talk to her, if you think that would help."

Betty frowned and said, "No, I'll be fine on my own." She climbed out of the car and headed inside to hash things out with her sister. I kept an eye just in case she wanted reinforcement.

After about 15 minutes, I was getting worried. There was no screaming or yelling. As her husband, I'd help Betty bury Sophia's body. I hoped that they hadn't strangled each other in there, but it was hard to tell. Because I had grown up an only child, I hadn't experienced sibling rivalry, but I had heard Betty tell stories about how she and her sister would get into nasty arguments; the claws would come out, as they say.

Just then the side door opened. I could see Betty and Sophia hugging in the doorway. Sophia headed towards her car with her head down. "Everything okay?" I called out to her. Not that I particularly cared, but I wanted to keep the peace.

Sophia eyed me up and down. That woman never liked me. Back then, I suspected that she didn't think I was good enough for her sister, but she never did say that to my face. "Yeah, we're good." She kept walking, avoiding me. She had always been such a sour thing.

That was a relief. I was still feeling a little bitter with her for upsetting Betty on our wedding day, but I decided to wait and talk to Betty myself. I didn't want to overstep.

Sophia's footsteps stopped crunching in the snow. "Wait a second," she called out to me. "I forgot – I have something for you and your *wife*," I felt that she emphasized 'wife' with a hint of sarcasm.

"What's this?" I asked as she handed me an unwrapped box.

"It's a wedding gift," she huffed, looking at me as if I were stupid.

"What is it?" I asked, half expecting her to be giving us some hand-me-down.

"It's a ceramic Christmas tree," she stated matter-of-factly. "Isn't the picture on the box indication enough?" she asked with attitude.

I muttered, "Thanks." I wasn't a fan of knick-knacks, but it was the thought that counted, I supposed.

She stared me down, like a wild animal ready to fight. "You're welcome," she replied with obvious reservation. "I'm trying."

"Got it," I tucked the box under my arm and headed towards the house.

Sophia had always been a difficult person. I don't know what her problem was with me, but the tension had been palpable throughout the years. She and Betty had a love/hate relationship. Currently, Betty loves Sophia, since she is living with her instead of with me.

Bringing myself back to the present day, I steadied myself as I dug the last item out of the box. That dreadful ceramic Christmas tree, a token of Sophia's first meddling in our relationship. After everything I had been through with Betty, trying to talk to her and work things out, Sophia finally got her wish and came between us. I shook my head. This damn tree was nothing but trouble. The tree was like a cockroach surviving the atomic bomb, and so was Sophia.

I grasped my hands around the pointed green edges of the ceramic tree and marched over to the trash can. I stomped on the foot pedal, and the lid flew open. I took pleasure in dropping that relic into the garbage and closing the lid. "Enough of that." I clapped my hands.

Just as I was done cleaning up, the landline rang. When I lifted the receiver, I felt joy when I heard the voice at the other end.

"Hey, Dad. How've you been? I've been thinking of you." My sweet daughter.

"Hi honey, I'm doing good. I've been thinking of you, too." And with that, I told my daughter all about Father Erikson's advice about getting into the Christmas spirit. I reminisced about one of the happiest days of my life, or at least the second happiest day of my life to forming our beautiful family.

CHAPTER 30

WYATT

As soon as Dana left the shop, I locked the door. I leaned my back against the glass and slid halfway down. I hung my head until my chin touched my chest. I felt mentally and physically exhausted. Stress certainly takes its toll.

Dana was one of my best friends, but she could be exasperating. I knew that she meant well, and I did appreciate our heart-to-heart. As much as I complained that people meddle in my business, which, for the record, I hate, I do love Dana. She was the first woman I trusted after my mom left. It was hard letting someone in when you were concerned that they'd eventually up and leave you.

I feel bad for fibbing to her earlier, but I needed to do it. I've always loved Dana. Dana had been my first true love. She just didn't know it.

CHAPTER 31

Dana

I arrived at my shop late this morning because I made time to pop in to say 'Hello' to Marnie and grab a latte to go. After life-coaching Wyatt, I decided that I needed a caffeine fix to get me through the rest of the day.

Right on schedule, Sabrina burst through the door of my shop knocking over a bucket of thick birch bark sticks in the process. They tumbled noisily to the floor. Customers gazed in her direction, wondering what bull had just entered the flower shop.

"Look here!" she held up and waved a red envelope like a flag. "You've got mail!" She cajoled.

"Not another one!" I wailed. Who was taunting me? I wanted this madness to end.

"Could be. Or it could be a holiday card," she suggested. I grimaced as she flexed the envelope. I didn't want her to tamper with any evidence.

When she came near, I snatched it out of her hands. "Give it here!" I said, somewhat annoyed. I wasn't really mad at her. After all, she was only the messenger.

"What does it say?" Sabrina gazed over my shoulder and read the letter out loud:

Dear Dana,

Your smile both fills my heart and haunts me. I relive the last moment we shared every day of my life. I wish things had turned out differently. I'm sorry.

X

"Huh," Sabrina summarized my feelings exactly.

I could feel Sabrina's coffee-scented breath on my neck. I was growing increasingly agitated. "What?" I asked. My stomach was in knots at this point.

She took a finger out of her work glove and pointed to the letter. "Whoever it is, they're apologizing to you." Her eyebrows furrowed as she tried to think of who it could be. We both looked at each other, knowingly. There was someone I had hurt so badly, it was time to expose my deep, dark, not-so-secret confession: I broke someone's heart. No, I obliterated it.

CHAPTER 32

Reggie

Sophia got in the way – of course she did, but her meddling wasn't going to stop me. I had a new plan to connect with Betty.

I thought about what Wyatt had told me about the mysterious letters Dana was receiving. They sounded romantic. Was someone after her heart? I didn't want to get in the middle of things with Dana. She'd been through a lot with that former fella of hers who, if you ask me, could've treated her better. I never liked the guy, myself. Besides, she didn't need some old man butting into her personal life. Who was I to give anyone advice?

The more I thought about it, the more curious I was about how the letters made Dana feel. I wondered if I should do something similar for Betty.

I used to write letters to Betty when I was first courting her. I would slip a note into her purse or leave it in the rusty, old mailbox at the end of her driveway. It's the little things you do for one another that mean the most. Over the years, however, I stopped writing and, I guess, started taking her for granted. I forgot to keep courting my wife, to keep the romance alive.

A letter did sound romantic.

Maybe I should write Betty a love letter and reignite some sparks. Surely our old flame would stir some passion in her. Why not? What more could I lose?

I plunked myself down on the creaky, wooden chair in front of Betty's bureau. I rummaged through the drawers until I found some of her nice writing paper. Betty still preferred to send letters rather than emails to friends and family. I loved that about her.

I took out a sheet of crisp, white paper with lavender branches etched on the letterhead. I used to enjoy watching her when she'd fold the pages and seal them with care. She found a lot of joy meandering down to the post office, chatting up the locals, as she purchased her stamps. Whenever she received handwritten letters in the mail, usually from her friend, Alice, in Alberta, or her cousin, Sarah, in Newfoundland, her face would light up. She'd tear into those things like it was a gift on Christmas morning. She'd sit at her bureau and write back immediately to keep the pace of the conversation going.

Betty, I missed her.

I lifted the page to my face, inhaled her familiar scent, and my body relaxed. I held the paper to my chest and sighed. This has to work. I need my Betty back in my arms.

I laid the paper on the hard surface and steadied the pen, but when I went to start my letter to her, I froze. I didn't know what to say. After all my renewed enthusiasm to win her back, I was lost for words. I was paralyzed with anxiety.

What do I do? I was on the brink of losing the love of my life. If I couldn't write a letter professing my love, I was convinced that she wouldn't come back. I didn't know what to do. I stared helplessly at the blank page. Finally, I looked deep into my heart and wrote down the words that I should've been saying our entire married life.

CHAPTER 33

Wyatt

Before I get too ahead of myself, I should clarify that I've loved Dana like a *sister*, I still do, and I always will.

Once upon a time, before the *Winter Wonderland*, before the clammy hand in the cafeteria and even before 'show and tell,' I thought Dana was the coolest girl in the world.

I even remember some of our playdates when our moms were friends and would hang out. They'd sip their drinks—sometimes coffee, sometimes wine—while we'd run around the yard. Dana would pull worms out of the loose garden soil, shocked by how long they were. She wasn't afraid of getting dirt under her fingernails. By comparison, I was a menace. I'd cut them in half, just to see if they would slink away. Dana would laugh hysterically as we conducted our experiments. I've always loved adventurous women.

There were times when we'd find other creatures. A frog on the sidewalk? No problem! Dana mimicked their ribbits and held them in her small hands. I once dared her to kiss one to see if it would become a prince! She told me that kissing frogs, let alone boys, was gross. I couldn't argue with her about that. Once upon a time, we even wed in the schoolyard at recess; we really didn't know what 'getting married' meant. We thought it just made us the best of friends. When our classmates told me I had to kiss my bride, I shoved Dana into the dirt and ran in the opposite direction. Maybe marriage was never in my cards, not even as a kid.

When my mom left, right before Christmas, Dana and her family basically adopted me; their house was my second home growing up. I would be invited over for dinner, rides to soccer games, and sleepovers. I never knew if I was invited over because her mom felt sorry for me or if she was genuinely happy that her daughter had a best friend. Eventually, the sadness faded from her eyes, and I felt normal again – whatever 'normal' was.

Dana has always felt like more than just a friend to me—she had been like a sister, but not like Rachel. Dana has been someone I could rely on when the weight of the world felt unbearable, when nothing seemed to go my way, including failed grades, broken hearts, and the death of my grandparents. I particularly appreciated Dana during special occasions when I wished my mom could've been there, like Little League tournaments, birthdays, and graduations. Mom made her choice; she wasn't interested in our family anymore.

I remember the first time I allowed Dana to hug me after my mom left; there were few people I'd let in after the most important woman in my life up and left my family. When Dana hugged me, it felt like stepping into the warmth of a sunbeam after a long, cold night. Her hugs weren't just gestures; they were filled with an affection that wrapped around me like the coziest blanket, shielding me from the storm of emotions swirling inside. Believe me, a young man whose mom has left him stirs up a lot of different emotions. I've done my best to battle some of those demons, but a few of them still lurk in my mind.

I remember melting into Dana's arms, feeling a safety I didn't think I could find again. It wasn't easy to let someone in, especially when the person I trusted most in the world had walked away without warning. Love, of any sort, felt like a gamble I didn't want to take. She showed me, bit by bit, that being loved didn't always have to hurt and that it was okay to accept kindness without suspicion. In a way, I think Dana helped open my eyes to love with Sabrina all those years ago.

As we grew older, I will admit that I started to develop feelings for Dana. It was hard to explain exactly what it was – was it a friendship, love, or newly developed hormones acting up? It was difficult to say. I'll never admit it to her, ever, but when I reached across the table to hold her hand, I had cartoon hearts in my eyes. My pulse raced as I placed my hand on hers, hoping she'd return my affection. I bit my lip in anticipation, wondering if she felt the same.

But not all romances work out. When Dana recoiled from my touch in the cafeteria that day, I knew we were destined just to be friends. At first, I felt hurt by this. I hid from her for as long as I could to lick my wounds. I know it was foolish of me, but I was confused and hurt.

Dana will always be like a sister to me. Forever and always, I'll hold her dearly in my heart as family—even if she could at times be just as annoying as Rachel. And trust me, that's saying something because Rachel once spent an entire summer insisting that she could talk to squirrels. Spoiler alert: she couldn't. Dana, on the other hand, preferred her unique way of being insufferable: she'd provide relentless advice I didn't ask for and hugs I couldn't escape from, even if I wanted to. Spoiler alert: I didn't.

Despite the playful chaos, Dana has always been my constant. Through the highs, the lows, she's been there for me. She might drive me crazy sometimes, but that's what sisters do, right? And honestly, I wouldn't have it any other way.

Dana was special to me. She was the first woman I truly loved after my mom left—the first true love in my heart. I knew her first true love was someone else, and that was okay. Love isn't about being someone's everything; it's about cherishing them enough to never hurt their heart to heal your own.

CHAPTER 34
Dana

Devin. I never took the time to think about what happened between us. My wedding day behaviour broke his heart, not to mention publicly embarrassing him. For both of our sakes, I avoided thinking about that day.

Devin and I had casually dated in the last year of high school; I was still nursing a broken heart. By the time graduation rolled around, we had to decide whether to stay together in a long-distance relationship or to part ways. For those who choose the former option, the dreaded turkey dump often faces them when they return home for Thanksgiving. Having found a significant other, they break someone's heart, instead of a wishbone, and go back to school.

In our case, we found ourselves in the same city, an hour away from Mercer. He had a scholarship to play hockey in university, and I attended the local college to complete a business diploma. We coasted through school, and when Devin realized he couldn't pursue hockey further, we went back to Mercer so he could work at his father's car dealership. I was devastated. I wanted to leave this town and make something of myself. Dad always said it was better to leave and find yourself rather than to stay and never reach your potential. Those words stuck with me, tattooed on my mind.

Was I a failure because I didn't pursue my dreams by staying in the city to earn more business credits? I probably thought that Devin was the best that I could do. In some ways, I think I talked myself into staying with him: he was handsome, he was good to me, he had a car, and he had money, even if it was family money.

The first couple of years were okay. I took a job as a secretary at the dealership for Devin. We had our routine of going to the golf course on Wednesday nights to play a round with his work friends. On Saturdays, we watched sports at the pub and on Sunday, dinners were served at his parents' house. These were Devin's interests, not mine. I was slowly fading into his shadow.

On Valentine's Day, of all days, Devin asked me to marry him. If you asked me, I thought it was tacky of him. He made a big deal of the whole situation, but it was never about professing his love for me. In true Devin fashion, he made the entire proposal a spectacle. He found the one billboard in town, right on the highway, with a giant picture of himself holding open a red velvet box containing a large princess-cut diamond. He drove me there, during a snowstorm, to park in front of it for a minute to ask me to marry him. I had begged him not to drive out there, and in some way, Mother Nature was rooting for us not to work out, I see that now. Once we arrived at the billboard, he pulled out a small paper box with a microscopic diamond inside. He later gave me a cubic zirconia of the same ring on the billboard and said that was just for show. He had a reputation to uphold.

On the day of our wedding, which he planned, I got cold feet. It was a crisp fall day, and my cheeks stung with tears as I waited outside the church, deciding what to do. Sabrina, who never liked Devin, encouraged me to leave. "You don't have to do this," still rings in my ears. She had the keys to the getaway car. I was undecided about what to do. I couldn't keep up with that life anymore: existing behind a man who truly didn't see me as a person worthy of being loved.

Truthfully, I don't think I ever loved him, not in a way a lover should. He was a boyfriend decoy who, deep down, I knew that I didn't want in my life forever. My heart belonged to someone who had broken it years ago. I had just used Devin to get through my heartache.

It wasn't until the last minute that I made my choice and urged Sabrina to start the car. I knew that all the guests were seated in the chapel, that the music was about to begin, and that the bridal party was waiting for me to make an entrance. But I didn't want this wedding, this marriage, Devin. I chose to head for the hills. And I did.

I watched in slow motion as the smile slipped from Devin's face while he stood at the altar. I ran and slid into the passenger's side of Sabrina's car. Devin ran to the parking lot, but Sabrina gunned the engine and took off out of town.

Two weeks later I returned home. I was the talk of the town. Devin's father had fired me in a voicemail. My things had been thrown into black garbage bags and dropped off at my parents' house. When the dust finally settled, I opened *The Shrinking Violet* because I was done living in someone else's shadow. I wanted to step into the light of who I truly was—bold, imperfect, and unapologetically me. Choosing this life wasn't without its cost, but it felt necessary. Devin and I both had wounds to heal, apologies to offer, and two hearts that needed mending.

CHAPTER 35

Reggie

Dear Betty,

I've been a fool—a fool hopelessly in love with you from the moment we met. I still remember that day like it was yesterday: Mitch McDonald's party. You were the prettiest girl in the room, and your smile was all I could see. I was nervous about talking to you. You know I can be a bumbling fool. I knew I had to muster the courage to talk to you. And when I finally did, you stole my heart.

Since you've been gone, I've been haunted by every memory we shared— the good times and even the tough times (we've had our fair share of those, haven't we?). They play in my mind on a loop, reminding me of all the ways I fell short and all the reasons I need you back. I know I hurt you, Betty, and you have every right to be upset with me. But I have to ask—can you find it in your heart to forgive me?

I'm not perfect – never have been, never will be. But I'm trying to become a better man worthy of the love you've given me. I owe that to you and us.

I need to come clean. Maggie has been giving me ideas on how to woo you. I'm not always the best at gift giving. I hope you've enjoyed the surprises I've sent you. If I'm being honest, the best idea I ever had was asking you to be my wife. We vowed to stick together through the good times and the bad, and I know I haven't lived up to that promise as I should have. I could have been a better husband.

I've been trying, Betty. The flowers, the gifts—I hope they brought even a fraction of the joy you've brought to me. I've put my heart into each gesture, hoping you'd see how much I love you and how much I need you in my life.

I'm sorry for the times I let you down, for being a grumpy old man or distant when I should've been your rock. I'm a work in progress, and I promise you I'm working every single day to be the man you deserve. The man you first met, the man you married. I want to be that man to you again, and an even better version if you let me.

Bruce and I miss you more than words can express. This house isn't a home without you in it.

I've been thinking about our wedding day: the joy in your eyes, the love that filled the air; it reminded me of everything I'd give to have that with you again. Betty, I want to start over. I want to renew our vows and rebuild what we've always had.

If you meet me at 8 p.m. on Boxing Day, at the place we were married, I promise that I'll be there, ready to give you my all and to make you the happiest woman in the world.

Please, Betty. Say you'll be there.

With all my love,
Reggie

CHAPTER 36
Wyatt

"Hello, sailor!" Sabrina cooed in her best sultry voice as she burst through my front door. She leaned against the doorframe, peeling off her winter jacket like it was the hottest thing since sliced bread. Her very own attempt at a striptease, minus the music and with a lot more awkward shivering.

Rachel leapt from her corner of the couch. "Ew, gross. I'm in the room, people," she gagged, snatching up her laptop and making a beeline for the kitchen—her only safe haven from Sabrina's art of seduction.

Thank goodness for Sabrina, saving me from more quality time with Rachel. I didn't mind my little sister's company, except when the conversation circled back towards marriage. I wish she had a boyfriend I could hound her about and see how she feels.

Sabrina's mouth was wide open in a fake show of shock. "Was it something I said?" She clutched her invisible pearls. I couldn't help but laugh. I loved Sabrina's sense of humour and her ability to get under my sister's skin when the occasion arose. Rachel and Sabrina adored each other, but I enjoyed it when Sabrina joined forces with me instead.

I assured Sabrina, "Never mind her, she's a bit of a prude." She sauntered over and plunked herself down on the couch. I leaned over to kiss her. She moved towards me again to get another kiss. Her lips tasted like tangerines.

I smiled, thinking about our last trip down south to one of those all-inclusive hotels. I always think about being alone in paradise with Sabrina. She and I would sit on the beach all day drinking fruity cocktails with tiny, colourful umbrellas. At breakfast, when she thought no one was looking, Sabrina would stuff her pockets full of tangerines. When we sat poolside she'd pull out her citrus treats and devour them. And when I kissed her, I tasted paradise.

Damn, I loved this woman.

"What's on tonight?" Sabrina asked as she nuzzled up to me. She kissed the underside of my jaw; my five o'clock shadow had sprouted, scratchy to the touch. She loved to rub her face against my whiskers. I always thought it would hurt the delicate skin on her face, but she reassured me that she was fine; she just wanted to be close to me.

I wrapped my arms around her, drawing her closer. "We can watch whatever you want. I'm not fussy." I cocooned her in the blanket I had draped over my lap. I rested my face in her hair once we had settled into a cozy snuggle.

"Neither am I," she squeezed me tighter.

It wouldn't matter what we watched because five minutes later she was fast asleep.

Ever since Dana's sneak attack this morning, I have ruminated about my life: the past, the present and the future. I still had a lot on my mind, but one thing was for sure – Sabrina set my world on fire, in the best possible way. She was the love of my life.

With my beautiful girlfriend fast asleep beside me, I thought back to when we first met. There are days I think about our first encounter on repeat, like a pleasant dream.

Back then, when Dana didn't return my affections, I spent a lot of time alone. Being in junior high was torture enough, let alone being alone in junior high. Back then, Dana and I had our squabbles. To be honest, I wasn't entirely sure that I was going to make up with her after our falling out. My feelings had been hurt, and being a young man, I didn't know how to deal with my feelings. Some days, I still don't think I do. But I could just not get over losing my best friend.

When I saw Dana in the cafeteria with a new friend, I was momentarily jealous. She had obviously moved on. But how could she replace me? Then, one day, no sooner had I sat down when I heard Dana's voice call out to me, "Hey, Wy!" Dana was calling out and waving frantically to me, "Come join us." 'Us?' This so-called 'us' used to be her and me. I looked around nervously but decided to hide my feelings and join them. Secretly, I also wanted to suss out my replacement.

I headed to their table with a tray of piping hot poutine; I lived on fries and gravy for most of high school, too, and my face showed it. "Hey," I said awkwardly, avoiding Dana's gaze as I sat down. I needed a little time to warm up to the idea of being friends with her again, if we were ever going to be friends again.

Dana let out an exasperated sigh, "This is Sabrina," and she pointed towards a girl I had never seen before. "This is my best friend, Wyatt," she added. I looked up to meet Sabrina's eyes, and the magic began. I could've sworn that the butterflies had ripped through my stomach and fluttered out of my body.

"Hey," Sabrina said with a crooked smile. Her green and blue elastics somehow lit up her entire face under the fluorescent cafeteria lights.

My face reddened. "Hey," I echoed. I had a hard time thinking of anything else to say to this beautiful girl.

I knew she was special; I just didn't know how much at that moment. All at once, I forgot about my issues with Dana.

I remember reaching my hand out towards Sabrina, "Nice to meet you," I stuttered. My hand was cold and clammy from nerves and likely iron deficiency.

"Nice to meet you, too," Sabrina returned my introduction. "Cool t-shirt. I love that band," I had an 80s rock band plastered across my chest.

"Thanks," I continued to shake her hand beyond the socially accepted timeframe. I could feel my hands become moist with sweat, but she didn't make any effort to release my hand from hers. "They're my favourite band," I said shyly.

"Cool," she gazed into my eyes.

"Hello!" a muffled voice called out to us. "Earth to Wyatt," Dana was like the annoying little sister I already had. "I'm here too, you know." Her voice turned crystal clear, coming back into range.

When lunch was over, I boldly handed Sabrina a note with my phone number on it. "Text me sometime," I said, trying to act cool as I gave it to her, but cool really wasn't in my DNA. "If you want," I added nervously. She took the note from me, blushed and ran off to her next class when the bell rang.

Later that night, Sabrina texted me. She told me how much she liked meeting me and hoped that we could hang out sometime after school. I was smitten. Who would've thought that the girl who nearly stole my best friend would end up stealing my heart?

"What's that smile for?" Sabrina's groggy voice called out to me, tethering me back to the present.

I kissed her forehead. "Just thinking about the day we met,"

"Oh, you." Sabrina squeezed me tighter, and her sleepy eyes remained closed. "Always the romantic."

"It was one of the best days of my life, how could I forget it?" I kissed her forehead.

"It was the best day, wasn't it?" she replied.

"*One* of the best," I corrected her. "I think that there will be many more 'best' days to come." Sabrina rubbed her weary eyes and gave me the sweetest, longest kiss I think I've ever had in my life.

Yes, there would be many more amazing days ahead of us. I truly believed so.

CHAPTER 37

Dana

If I was ever going to clear the air with Devin, it was now or never. I had spent the past year doing my best to avoid him, for both our sakes. I decided that it wouldn't be fair to ambush him at work. He didn't deserve that. So, I did the next best thing and ambushed him at home.

My car lurched down the road, a few minutes out of town, past the old billboard Devin used to propose to me. I drove around the half-moon driveway and parked in front of the house that would have been our home.

Our home, if I hadn't gone and screwed everything up.

Devin's black SUV was parked out front, the trunk lid open and a pile of suitcases stacked inside.

"Hello?" I called out as I walked towards his house. The cold air nipped at my lips, stinging the chapped corners. "Devin?"

"Who is it?" I heard his muffled voice from behind a stack of brightly coloured gifts. He stopped in his tracks to see who'd shown up at his abode. When he lowered the boxes and took a good look at me, the smile faded from his face. "Oh, it's you."

Ouch, that stung, but his response wasn't all that surprising. I supposed I was the last person he'd expected to see at his home.

"It's me!" I extended my arms out to the side, as if I were the star on top of the Christmas tree, my face brightly lit. "How are you?" I asked a little too enthusiastically. "It's been a while!" I was trying too hard. I felt the sweat against my body turn icy cold.

He looked away from me, obviously irritated. "Well, it's been 14 months, but who's counting?" He dropped the gifts in the trunk with a thud. "What do you want?" Devin cut to the chase. He definitely wasn't in the mood for a social visit.

My smile started to fade. "I wanted to see how you are…" I trailed off when he glared at me.

He crossed his arms over his navy blue pea coat. "You should've thought when you left me at the altar."

For a moment, I thought that my heart had stopped beating. "I didn't mean to do that to you," I shrank. I felt awful, but I tried my best not to think about the hurt he must have gone through.

"You've had quite a while to say something," he scolded me. His steely blue eyes met mine momentarily and looked away. I ached, feeling his pain and anger towards me, but I was on a mission.

I thought I should go out on a limb, to see if once and for all, Devin was the author of those letters. "Does my smile haunt you?" I tiptoed into unknown territory. Surely Devin was the one who sent me these letters. Love and hate ran a fine line between each other.

"I'd say you haunt me alright," he mumbled.

Unsure whether I had heard him correctly, I dared to venture, "Do you miss me?" my voice probing for answers I wasn't sure I wanted. As much as I craved his response, I silently hoped it would confirm what I was pretty certain that I already knew—that we weren't right for each other. Still, I needed to know if he was the one sending the letters, if only to put an end to it once and for all.

A look of horror spread across his face. "Do I miss you? After what you did to me? I should think not!" he bellowed, slamming his fist against the vehicle.

I couldn't help but jump.

"You embarrassed me in front of nearly the entire population of Mercer!" Devin had been holding this in for the last 14 months, and I deserved to get an earful from him for what I did.

"I was upset too! Far more than you realize." I shot back. I was on rockier ground than I initially thought. I don't know why I decided to try to fight back. What was the point? We had both hurt each other.

He looked around at no one in particular. I could have sworn I saw steam coming out of his ears.

I thought about who I'd become over the last year and what I'd accomplished. Part of me pushed to become the person I am today because of Devin, for better or for worse. "You never appreciated me for me." A weight, which I didn't know was there, was lifted off my chest.

For once in his life Devin was lost for words. "Yes, I did," he contended at an inaudible volume. He sounded like a hurt child.

"How?" It was my turn to be wounded.

"I," he searched for the memories, the words to defend his honour, but came up with nothing. We stood there for a few minutes, looking at each other, lost in the hurt we both caused, searching for a way out.

"I'm sorry I hurt you," I started. He deserved an apology. No one should ever go through that. "I'm sorry that I embarrassed you. We should have spoken in private rather than me taking off." As much as I had appreciated Sabrina and her getaway car at the time, it wasn't the right thing to do. It was, however, the easiest thing to do at the time. I had taken the coward's way out. It was something I wasn't proud of, but I had to live with it.

"You think," he pouted. I deserved that.

After an awkward delay, he added, "I'm sorry, too. I wasn't aware that you didn't feel appreciated." I felt as if he had finally heard me. Then, he ruined the moment by saying, "But you should have said something. I'm not a mind reader."

We both stared at each other. Time stood still. The only thing that could be heard was the whistling wind. Our chapter was finally closed.

"I moved on," he finally said.

I couldn't help but feel a little ache in my heart. "I heard." For what it was worth, I had loved him, even if it was for a moment in time. "Tiffany is a great person."

He cleared his throat. "We're headed to her parents' house to have an early Christmas. Then we're headed to the Bahamas for the holidays." He slammed the trunk shut. "I'm going to ask her to marry me."

"Oh, wow," I couldn't help but be shocked. He moved on fast, and I hadn't even attempted to move on, at least not romantically.

He quickly went in for the kill. "What? You didn't want to marry me. I wasn't going to wait forever."

"I didn't mean it like that." Well, I kind of did mean to judge him. He was never the type of guy to be single for long.

Our conversation, though short, was a long time coming. I realized that this deep, dark secret wasn't as harsh as I thought it was for this past year. People in town cast their judgment on me for leaving my fiancé at the altar. Even Devin had moved on. People change; life goes on. I knew I wasn't likely to ever get the closure I thought I needed from Devin, but this was a start. The next step was to forgive myself and to finally move on with my life.

Lost in my thoughts, I didn't at first hear an angry, high-pitched voice yelling at me. It wasn't until Devin rushed towards the front porch that I finally clued in.

"Hey! Get away from him!" Devin caught Tiffany as she tried to lunge off the porch in her fuzzy pink slippers. "You've already caused him enough problems! Get out of here!"

"I'm leaving!" I cried out as I stumbled over the snowbank towards my car. Just as I wrenched the door open, something narrowly missed my head. I reached into my hair and realized there was a clump of snow matted in it.

Then, another strike hit my driver's side window. I slowly raised my head to see what danger lay on the other side, other than an angry girlfriend and a jilted ex-fiancé. I ducked just in time as Tiffany hurled another snowball at me. She meant business.

"I said get out of here!" she wailed. She was protective of her partner. I hoped that he treated her better than he did me. My guess was that he might be a bit scared of her, and I wouldn't blame him.

"Tiffany, stop!" I heard him plead with her.

I revved the engine and skidded out of the driveway as fast as I could. I gave Tiffany what she wanted, for me to leave her boyfriend alone. And, in a few days, he'd make her the blushing bride that I never was.

CHAPTER 38

Reggie

As soon as I put the pen down, I felt my body relax. I smoothed my hands over the letter. I had one final prayer that my wish would come true. I had done all that I could, and it was time to see how Betty would respond. The ball was in her court, as they say.

Before putting my plan into action, there was one more thing to do. If I were inviting my bride to join me in renewing our vows, I didn't want her to stress out about what to wear. Betty would look beautiful in anything, but I knew she had a few favourites, most women do. I headed straight for her wardrobe, took hold of the brass knobs and opened the doors. I sorted through the garments to find just the right item for the Boxing Day vow renewal, if she shows up.

Then, I found it. Her sapphire blue dress. It wasn't the traditional white dress, like in our wedding photo, but it didn't matter. Betty and I were married, already bound together in ways that went deeper than any fancy ceremony. I carefully took the dress off the hanger and headed toward the bed, knowing that this would speak louder than any words could.

I gently folded the dress in a sheet of fresh, crisp tissue paper and placed it in a box that I had found on the wardrobe shelf. Just then,

Bruce jumped onto the bed. I couldn't risk getting cat hair on my precious package and said, sternly, "Not now, cat!" The little devil hissed at me in retaliation.

I sighed, as I usually do these days. "I'm sorry, Bruce. This is for Betty." I tried to coax him to come near me, but he batted at me. A low yowl reverberated throughout his tiny body.

"I'm just trying to do something nice for your mother," I shook my head at him. Were pet parents *really* a thing? Betty seemed to think so.

After a few moments, Bruce came towards me and let me pet his head. He purred as I stroked his fur, throwing his body up against my thigh. I think he forgave me, but it's hard to tell with these temperamental beasts. Perhaps he got it from me. What is it that they say, nature versus nurture? Anyway, I didn't have time for any of that psychology nonsense.

I left my furry pet behind as I took the box to the kitchen, securing the note that I had already written on top. No sooner did I finish getting things together than the doorbell rang. I know I had apologized to Father Erikson, but I hoped those kids weren't back for more songs. I'd say 'I'm sorry' a thousand times if it meant they never sang me another note.

A blast of cold air shot through the house as I opened the door. "Wyatt stood there with a wide smile on his face. "Hey Reggie, everything ready?" he asked. Thank goodness it was him.

"Just a minute," I said as I retreated into the house to fetch the parcel that he had come to pick up. "It's all done." I handed him the box and clapped my hands together. Whatever would be would be. My plan was now in motion. A weary smile formed on my lips, but I quickly brushed it off to save face in front of the young man.

"Great," I'll drop it off. I've got the address loaded on my GPS.

"Thanks again, Wyatt. You've been a great, uh, friend." I looked down at my feet, embarrassed. I didn't have many friends, real friends, anyway.

It seemed that the feeling was mutual since Wyatt's face turned crimson. He tugged at the sherpa-lined collar of his winter coat. "Anytime," he commented as he headed back towards his car.

"Oh!" I called out after him. "By the way, Sophia has a gun collection. You'd best be careful when you set foot on her property!" I waved as he turned to look at me, panic-stricken.

"What?" He choked out, his eyes wide with fear.

"Have a safe drive!" I called out and slammed the door. At least it wasn't me setting foot in the dragon's den again. I'll pray for you, Wyatt Greene, you'll need it.

CHAPTER 39

WYATT

I was reluctant to leave Reggie's stoop after he warned me about his sister-in-law owning guns. Was she a hunter? Or was she into some doomsday theory? I tried ringing Reggie's doorbell again, but he didn't answer.

When I got into my car, I saw the ginger cat perched in the window, slinking down like he was monitoring the street. Behind him, I could've sworn I saw Reggie cower. I'll have a chat with him when I get back.

I followed the route, just like Reggie said, and pulled up a long driveway. I parked in front of a rundown house. I looked down at my phone to check the address he'd sent me. "This must be the place," I mumbled to myself.

I reached across to the passenger seat and picked up the box he had sent with me. I wondered what he had for Betty. Apparently, Juan, or someone from the yard, who usually dropped things off, wasn't available, so I was the next choice. Reggie said that he'd do it himself, but he ran into issues with Betty's sister and he hoped that a stranger stopping by might have better luck.

As I got out of the car, the cold air nipped at my nose. I tucked the parcel, with the attached letter, under my arm and made my way up the steps. Just as I reached the top, a storm door opened, and an older woman emerged with a lit cigarette dangling out of her mouth. This had to be the dreaded Sophia.

"Hold it right there, young fella." She took a long draw on her cigarette and asked not so politely, "What do you think you're doing here?" As she looked me over, I couldn't help but shudder. I felt like a piece of meat!

I held the box out in front of me. "This is for Betty." The parcel shook in my hands, rustling the contents.

"Oh lord. Not another one." Reluctantly, Sophia took the box from me, the cigarette now smouldering between her fingers. "Let me guess who it's from." She tapped her lip, in mock thought.

"Santa, of course!" I tried to make light of the situation.

"Ha!" She let out a smoker's cough. "If Santa was a deadbeat husband, maybe," Sophia sneered as she tossed the box into a snow-covered patio chair.

I tried to back up. This delivery was becoming too confrontational for my liking. My mind raced to some scary possibilities. Before anything bad happened, the storm door opened again, and this time Betty emerged. She said, "Sophia! What are you doing to that poor young man?"

Sophia scoffed. "Nothing yet," she smiled as she gave me another once over.

The two sisters spoke quietly to one another. I couldn't hear much of what they were saying, but it was clear that Betty wanted to hear me out.

Once Sophia went back inside Betty asked, "Wyatt, what are you doing here?"

I collected Reggie's parcel and said, "I'm here to bring you this." I motioned towards the box I was holding.

"Another one," she said. Silence hung in the cold air. And then, she asked, "How is the old fool?" A sad smile turned up the edges of an otherwise frown.

I shrugged, "I'm not sure. All I know is he misses you."

Betty rolled her eyes and made an inaudible comment. I sensed the sadness in her eyes.

"What's he been up to," she asked, "besides sending me all this stuff? Is he trying to tell me that he's a changed man?"

"He might be." Then, I added awkwardly, "Maybe you should read the note on the parcel.

Betty reached for it and took it between her fingers. "And what if he's not?" She asked.

"Reggie is a good man. He loves you."

Betty said nothing in return.

"He is lost without you," I added, struggling for words.

Betty huffed.

"What do you love most about Reggie?" Betty shot a glance at me. My unexpected question hung in the air.

"Why do you ask me that?"

"I'm thinking about getting married myself, and I can't help wondering if it is a good idea. How can you and Reggie be married for so long, and have a falling out at this stage in your relationship?"

"We only had a falling out because he doesn't appreciate me," Betty replied.

"He's not perfect, that's for sure." I offered. Betty laughed.

"I admit that Reggie has always provided for our family. He has given me a beautiful home, a wonderful daughter and food on the table. I've never gone without, but there's more to a marriage than that."

"So, being a provider isn't enough?" I asked. Sometimes I worried; Sabrina had a good paying job, and she made more money than I did. She never rubbed it in, but I still wondered if I could provide for her. "That's what a man is supposed to do, isn't it?"

Betty shrugged her shoulders, "No, that's not all." She clasped her hands together. "Reggie doesn't say he appreciates me enough, even though I know that he does. There are times he'll stop by a farmer's stand on his way home from work and buy me a bouquet of wildflowers. Sometimes, when we go out to dinner, he'll save his after-dinner mint for me because he knows how much I love them. If we go to the movie theatre, he always lets me have the aisle seat so I can stretch out my legs; my knee has been giving me grief since my surgery. It's the little things he does that tell me he loves me. But a person needs to hear those things occasionally, too." She shrugged, momentarily lost for words and then resumed talking, "Sometimes he can be crabby and get on my nerves. I know I can act that way, too. No one's perfect," she laughed.

"I know that words are important," I replied. Doing nice things for Sabrina also tended to be the way I showed how much I cared for her because it was hard at times to put my feelings for her into words.

"What are you going to do now?" I asked Betty.

"Well, I guess I'll read what Reggie has to say and go from there." She waved the envelope in her hand. I wondered what he wrote.

"What about you? What are you going to do?" she asked me in return.

"I don't know yet. I love Sabrina, and she loves me."

"That's a start," Betty cut in. "Love is the secret sauce of marriage."

As I returned to my vehicle, I heard Betty call out, "Good luck to you, Wyatt. Whatever you decide to do, that will be the right decision for you."

CHAPTER 40

Dana

"Wow, that's some story," Sabrina commented when I told her about the day's events. I purposefully neglected to tell her about my earlier confrontation with Wyatt. He and I both agreed to keep that conversation to ourselves; no need to upset Sabrina.

Sabrina took a piece of tape and stuck it between her fingers as she sealed the paper seam on a sweater she was wrapping as a gift for her dad. "So, it's not Bryan," she smoothed her fingers over the gift wrapping.

"Nope," we both shuddered. To me, his incessant talking would be a fate worse than death. Even Rachel was trying to avoid him since she's been home.

"Good, because my Christmas wish for you would be for you to go permanently deaf if you married him." Sabrina caught herself in a giggle.

"That's not very nice," I smiled coyly as I took a sip of my hot chocolate. Ruby curled up at my feet and sighed, enjoying her mostly silent night. I needed to find her the best dog dad, if I were ever to marry.

"And it's not Devin." She folded an end into a crease, placing the finishing touches on the parcel. She did everything with such precision that she could have become a surgeon.

My body relaxed, "Nope, not him either." I reached over and felt the sparkling piece of tinsel dangling from the tree beside me. "I'm happy he's moved on," even if it was with loony tunes Tiffany.

Sabrina glanced at me, studying my face. I knew that she was worried about me since I left him. I hoped she'd worry no more after I had seen him and cleared the air today. He was finally in my life's rearview mirror.

"I still don't know who it is." I tapped my finger against my lips. I'd run out of options at that point. Maybe the letters were just a joke, someone playing a prank on me.

A sinister smile spread across Sabrina's face. "Maybe it's the Thompson boy after all!" She jested, "Maybe you could be his sugar mama!" I whipped a candy cane throw pillow in her direction, knocking her newly wrapped gifts off the coffee table.

"Santa is watching," she warned me, replacing the gifts back onto the table. "He won't bring you a boyfriend with that attitude." Sabrina comically wiggled her eyebrows.

"Shut up!" I laughed at her. I wasn't sure if I even wanted a boyfriend. If I wished for one, I'm sure he'd get stuck in the chimney, or worse- no gift receipt if I didn't like him!

She lay down on the floor to pet Ruby, "You love me dearly, you know." My geriatric baby rolled over to show her belly and to accept more pets from Sabrina, whom I lovingly referred to as Ruby's godmother.

"Yeah, yeah. I love you." Sabrina was like a sister to me. She always had my best interests at heart, even if she got on my nerves from time to time.

And, as the night went on, I decided to put the letters out of my mind and focus on finishing up for the holiday. Tomorrow would be a great day to finalize holiday orders and join the others at the Christmas Eve Market.

Around midnight, I padded around the house, turning off the lights and then I let Ruby curl up at the edge of my bed. After all my sleuthing, and for the first time, I wanted to be close to someone. I didn't want to be alone anymore.

And, while I was dreaming, my secret admirer crept up to my house under the cover of darkness to deliver one last letter underneath my back door. I'd wake up tomorrow, read it and come to the realization that I had been wrong all along about who was in love with me. The answer couldn't have been more obvious.

Dear Dana,

My biggest regret in life was losing you. Let's make it right. Please meet me under the mistletoe at the Christmas Eve Market tonight.

X

CHAPTER 41

Reggie

Even though the skin didn't melt off my bones the last time I was at church, it didn't mean it wouldn't melt this time. As soon as I entered the building, I couldn't help but shudder. The things I was willing to do for love!

It was time to face what I was dreading most. I stood outside the dark confessional box, eyeing it suspiciously. I wasn't sure if I could go in or not. If I did, it would be like opening Pandora's box. No one would be ready for what was in my soul, and I was certainly sure there wasn't enough holy water to extinguish the flames I'd burst out in. Father Erikson had suggested that I try coming to confession to relieve myself of my sins and get forgiveness. The only person I wanted forgiveness from was Betty. He attempted to convince me, saying I'd feel a wave of calm wash over me, but I think I was starting to develop hives. I scratched at my irritated skin.

What was the point of all this nonsense? Why did I have to get inside this small closet to confidentially share my deepest, darkest secrets? The man of the cloth already knew me. What good would it do to share my feelings with him? I stared hard at the door to this portal of torture so long that Father Erikson opened his confessional box door to see what was going on. Perhaps he thought I took off. I wish I had.

"Everything alright, Reggie?" he asked with genuine concern. I'm not the type to open up, but the tone of his voice gave me the courage, although reluctantly, to go ahead with this unloading of my conscience. "I'm ready when you are." He eyed me before gently closing the door shut.

I took a deep breath, stepped inside and began, "Forgive me Father for I have sinned."

Out of the corner of my eye, I could make out the shadow of Father Erikson through the latticed opening. There didn't seem to be anything judgmental about his face, and he was just quietly waiting for me to start confessing. I took a deep breath. I knew that I could do this even though my nerves were kicking in.

"Follow me." He began, "First, make the sign of the cross." Which we did together. That was easy enough. I could get the hang of this.

"Then, repeat after me: Bless me, Father, for I have sinned." I dutifully repeated after him. "Very good," Father Erikson said.

"Now, you say: 'My last confession was...'" and I repeated after him, word for word, just like he asked. When I was done, there was only silence.

After what seemed like an eternity, Father Erikson asked, "When was your last confession?" he was puzzled by my lack of reply. He probably wasn't going to like what I had to say next.

I sat there thinking back. When *was* my last confession? For the life of me, I couldn't think of it. I shrugged my shoulders in the dark and said, "Maybe never?" which was the truth. I couldn't recall a time in my life when I had stepped into this wooden cupboard to bare my soul.

"Not even when you and Betty got married?" he asked.

"Well," I thought back, "maybe, but that's a lifetime ago. I don't remember what I had for breakfast," I chuckled nervously. And that was true. I had a mind like a sieve.

"You've never confessed to anyone, ever?" Try as I might, I could not recall ever having gone to confession.

"I suppose you could say the boys at *Lucky's Pub* know a thing or two about me, or Lou's boy. He's become a bit of a friend these days." I tried to think a little harder. Surely, I've confided in someone. Then it struck me. Yes, of course, him! How could I forget? "Of course, there's Bruce. He knows *everything* about me," I said with as much sincerity as I could muster, "especially over the last few months since Betty left." Bruce had become an important part of my bachelor lifestyle.

"Reggie, your cat doesn't count!"

The lattice woodwork cast a shadow upon my face. "Father Erikson," I started to panic. Maybe this was a mistake, "I don't think that confessing is going to work for me." Anxiety flooded my brain. I got up to leave. The wooden seat creaked as I stood.

"Patience, my son," brought me back to my seat.

Ever so slowly, I began to release all that was pent up inside, things that I didn't even realize were lurking in the back of my mind. I wasn't sure what powers he had, but when I started to share all the things I had been hesitant to share, even with people I trusted, I felt the tension in my body vanish. At the end of confession, Father Erikson gave me my penance. A sense of calm washed over me. I was going to win Betty back. I just felt it.

CHAPTER 42

WYATT

"Big brother, you're home!" Rachel squealed. She was in the kitchen baking up such a storm that the fire alarm had gone off. She was in the process of waving her arms in a vain attempt to make the thing stop.

"Here, let me." I offered. Rachel plunked the oven mitt into my hand. I fanned the smoke until the alarm finally silenced.

"You came home just in time. So much for my gingerbread," she said with a shrug of her shoulders. "Though I would have settled for some hot firemen if you hadn't come home." She stifled a laugh. What was with women and firemen, anyway?

"Glad I could be of service," I tossed the oven mitt down and headed for the fridge. "Although most of the firemen here are bald with beer bellies, if that's your thing." Rachel rolled her eyes at me. "Why are you making all of this stuff?" I asked as I cracked open a beer.

"I wanted to do something nice for you and Dad. Is that a crime?" She put her hands on her hips and threw me a threatening look.

"Just don't burn the next batch." I moved quickly out of the kitchen to dodge a burnt gingerbread man flying in my direction.

Enough of Rachel and her tantrums. I reached into my pocket for my phone. I wanted to text Sabrina about ordering a pizza tonight. When I reached in, I realized that it wasn't there.

"Damn it," I cursed.

"What's wrong, crybaby?" Rachel mocked me.

"Get a life," I barked back at her.

"I have one, why don't *you* get a life?"

"I have to go back to the shop." I set my untouched beer down. "I forgot my phone."

"How convenient, and just when I wanted to spend some quality time with my big brother," she replied sarcastically.

"I'll be back," I said. "In the meantime, if you need some companionship, why don't you just start another fire?" Rachel groaned loudly as I slammed the door on my way out.

When I pulled up to the shop, the parking lot was empty, and the lights were off. I unlocked the back door and made my way inside. A dim light coming from underneath my dad's office door stopped me in my tracks. I'm certain that I turned the lights off when I left earlier. I moved slowly towards the door. The faint sound of music was coming from inside the office. "What the hell?" I whispered to myself. Who could be here?

I grasped the handle door. I steadied my hand, preparing for what was inside. I took three deep breaths and quietly turned the knob before ramming the door wide open. I was definitely *not* prepared for what I saw.

Two roundish, white spheres were shimmying back and forth. I swore I was witnessing an eclipse. "What the hell?" I croaked, realizing that I was looking at someone's buttocks.

Shocked, my dad turned around. "Wyatt! What are you doing here?" In a panic he grabbed a nearby Christmas stocking to cover his exposed chestnuts. Too late for that!

"I could ask you the same thing!" I said, shocked beyond belief at what I was seeing.

In all of the commotion I hadn't noticed who else was in the room with him. Perched on the office sofa in all her glory was none other than Marnie, who was laughing uncontrollably.

"Wyatt, we can explain," Marnie said, trying unsuccessfully to stifle her laughter.

"Yes, son. We can explain," my dad piped in.

Then it hit me. The playful interaction in the café made sense – my dad and Marnie were dating!

"Nope, I'm good," I said, trying to unsee what I just saw. "We don't need to talk about this." I tried to back out of the office, bumping into everything behind me.

"Really, son, we wanted to talk about this. We were just waiting for the right time." My dad pleaded.

"Well, I'm an adult, so, any time is a good time." With that, I turned to make a hasty exit.

"Wyatt, please," Marnie pleaded.

But, instead of listening, I made a beeline for the parking lot.

CHAPTER 43

Dana

"I don't remember delivering it," Sabrina said, studying the fourth and final message.

"That's because you didn't. It was at my house this morning. Someone left it there." I took a swig of coffee. I had a pile of mistletoe wrapped and ready to take to the market tonight.

"Who could it be?" I could see Sabrina searching her mental Rolodex of men in Mercer. With each shake of her head, it was as if she was striking one at a time from her list – but then she stopped. "You don't think it could be," she hesitated, unsure if she should continue.

I stared at her, wide-eyed, waiting for her to finish her sentence. Her dramatic effect sometimes made my fragile heart stop beating.

She mouthed the name *Tom*.

My heart ached. Of course, I forgot about him.

Tom.

I haven't thought of him in years. Well, that's not true. I had thought of him with a painful longing.

He was the one who got away.

I never recovered from it.

CHAPTER 44

Reggie

I decided to pick up the last car part I had ordered and work on my project over the holiday before going back to the lumber yard in the new year. The distraction of working on my prized possession was what I needed just now. I still hoped to have the car done by the summer so that Betty and I could cruise around town in it. When I closed my eyes, I could almost feel the wind blowing in our hair, the warm sun on our faces as we weaved along the country roads. That was but a dream.

I pulled into the parking lot, swung my legs out of the truck and jumped down. My feet landed on the frozen ground with a dull thud. Pain shot up through my legs, making my lower back ache. I could swear that at one point I was still able to reach the ground from the truck with ease. Maybe I've been shrinking, but what I knew for sure was that my body wasn't getting any younger; I'd probably feel this pain for days.

There was hardly anyone in the shop. Christmas music was blaring. I was looking forward to the holidays being over.

Bloody Christmas!

The shop was like a second home, aside from the poor taste in music. I preferred the sound of machinery and the smell of oil in the air. Damn, that smelled good, almost intoxicating. It probably wasn't healthy to breathe all this stuff in, but something would kill me eventually, so long as it wasn't Sophia. I couldn't wait to pick up my part and head home; I needed the distraction, something to fill my cup, so to speak. The anticipation of Boxing Day and Betty's lack of response to my wooing was wreaking havoc on my nerves.

Loud footsteps echoed on the tiled floor. "Ah, I thought I heard the door chime." Lou popped out from the office to greet me. "What can I do for you, Reggie?"

We shook hands and I said, "Just stopping by to see if the part I ordered was in." I can't recall if Lou ever got remarried after his wife left. Unlike women, men don't talk about that kind of thing. I glanced at his left hand looking for a wedding ring, but I didn't see one. I supposed he was still a bachelor. I looked up at him.

Lou patted his hand on the countertop. "I'll look in the back. Hold tight."

He had done well for himself. Besides running a successful business, he had raised two kids on his own. He looked in good health and spent most of the time working with his son. There was nothing wrong with that. I sure would like to spend more time with my daughter, but I don't think she'd want to work in the lumber yard, although there were enough fools hurting themselves. I'm sure she could nurse them back to health.

As I waited, I wondered just what had happened to Lou's wife so many years ago. Carol was her name. One day she bolted out of town and never came back. Those poor kids of theirs learned to adapt to life with only a father figure. Back then, people just let sleeping dogs lie.

They didn't ask questions. They didn't judge. That's who people are in a small town like Mercer.

I wondered if Betty would end up leaving me, just like Lou's wife had done. She's already moved out of town, so what was all that different? Lou was a kind man. I hoped he would find someone special, one day. He deserved it. As for me, maybe I was destined to be alone for the rest of my life. I certainly hoped not.

Love is so precious and so fickle.

Lou interrupted my daydreaming when he came back into the room. "Here's your order." He placed the cardboard package on the counter and punched something into the computer. I fished my wallet out of my jacket pocket and dutifully handed over my credit card for processing. "Anything else I can do for you?" Lou asked, smiling from ear to ear. This guy always seemed so happy. I wondered what his secret was. How could anyone be this happy when they're alone?

"Is Wyatt here, by chance?" I needed to talk to him. The sooner the better.

"Wyatt?" Lou asked nervously, as if he had another son. "Yes, he's just on his break," he threw his thumb behind him, signalling that Wyatt was in the break room. "I'll get him for you." He turned and started to walk away, though it looked like he'd rather stay with me.

"No need, I know where the breakroom is." I started to head down the hallway with a slight limp. My legs were still giving me grief. "Oh, and Lou, if I don't get a chance to see you before the holiday, Merry Christmas."

"Thanks, Reggie. You, too," he said over his shoulder as he disappeared into his office.

I nudged the break room door open. Wyatt was sitting at the table, deep in thought, with a take-out bag from the *Bean There, Done That* sitting in front of him.

"Reggie," he said as he set his sandwich onto the brown paper wrapper. "What are you doing here?"

I ignored his question. Time was of the essence. "Wyatt, my friend. How are you?" I tried to sound cheery, but I was concerned about how he was after coming face to face with the dragon lady, Sophia. He sat there, stone-faced and unresponsive.

"So, how was the drive?" I tried again, but why wasn't Wyatt taking the conversational bait?

"You can cut the small talk," Wyatt said as he crossed his arms over his chest. His untouched sandwich sat in front of him. "I'm traumatized."

"What happened?" I felt a lump in my throat, anticipating the worst.

He narrowed his eyes at me and shook his head. "I had no idea what I was getting into when you asked me to make that delivery."

But I wasn't about to be sidetracked. "About Betty?" I asked. I needed to know how she had received my latest offering, whether she had even got it. I knew that he was upset about the reception he undoubtedly received when he drove up to Sophia's house, where Betty was staying. I tried to laugh off her eccentric behaviour, but he was having none of that.

"I did warn you about her," I stuttered.

"That's not exactly true," he replied, obviously annoyed with me.

"You didn't tell me that she was a man-eater." Wyatt's face turned red. He looked away. Was he embarrassed with himself?

I hadn't said that she could devour half of a dead turkey at Thanksgiving by herself, let alone a full-grown adult man, but maybe I should've. "What did the old battle axe do?" I whispered across the table, trying to play the sympathy card.

Wyatt turned his gaze away from me. "I've witnessed things I wish never to experience again," I swear I saw his bottom lip quiver.

Oh, boy. I was beginning to regret involving him in my predicament.

There weren't any more words that needed to be spoken. Men don't talk openly about their worst experiences, especially ones that in hindsight they feel that they could have managed better.

I shook the chill out of my bones. "Listen, I was wondering if I could ask another favour of you." I didn't want to meet his eyes, still feeling sheepish about asking him to get involved in my affairs in the first place and especially after what he just endured with my despicable sister-in-law.

Wyatt's eyes grew wide with panic. "Another one?" he said, shocked. "I'm not going back there! I'm not, Reggie! There's no way in hell!"

I tried to reassure him that this request wouldn't be as upsetting, but I could appreciate his hesitation.

I dared to try again. "Just this one more favour, please," I begged. I tried to smile cheerfully at him, to put him at ease. "You can say no, but I hope you won't. Everything is riding on this."

After a brief pause, he said, "What is it?" Wyatt's voice was monotone and unimpressed. I was glad he was at least going to consider my request before shooting me down.

I scratched the stubble on my face. "I need help decorating the church for when Betty comes to town." That was my hope, but there was no guarantee of that happening. "If she comes to town on Boxing Day," I said.

He looked confused. "I thought the church was already decorated?"

"Yes," I hesitated, "but I want to add a few special details." I smoothed my hands across the table. "Would you consider helping an old man?" I prayed he would say yes.

Wyatt sat back in his chair and crossed his arms again, contemplating my request. "Do you think guilt tripping me will work?" he narrowed his gaze at me.

He wasn't wrong. I was trying to manipulate him. I began to feel very guilty, but what he said next surprised me.

"When do you need help?" he conceded.

I smiled, filled Wyatt in on the decorating details, and we called it a night. Wyatt had planned to pick up a few other items and come to the church when he was finished work when I needed him. I knew that I could count on him. I owed Wyatt big time.

Things were falling into place. There was reason for optimism. All I had to do now was wait for the big day- our 40th wedding anniversary; I couldn't believe it. Time flew by in an instant. I just hoped I still had an anniversary to celebrate when the day came. Betty still had time to mull things over and meet me at the church, that is, if she could still see a glimmer of our forever in the distance.

CHAPTER 45

Wyatt

I don't recall exactly how I got home from the shop. The drive back was a daze. My head was still spinning from what I had witnessed in Dad's office. As soon as I parked, I ran inside the house and looked for a place to hide; anywhere would do.

I had barely removed my coat when Rachel asked, "What's wrong with you?"

I stopped for a second to shoot daggers at her with my eyes. "Mind your own business!" My voice echoed down the hall as I ran to my bedroom and slammed the door shut like a moody teenager.

Rachel, who lacks boundaries, burst through the door. "Wyatt, what's up your butt?" she asked without any attempt at empathy.

"Leave me alone, twerp." My muffled voice called out from under the pillow I had lodged my head under.

Rachel jumped on the bed, testing the springs and my patience. "You're so lame!" she said mockingly.

"What are you, 12?" I tried to throw a spare pillow at her. I missed, knocking a few superhero collectables off my bookshelf. "Ugh!" I groaned. Nothing was going my way at the moment.

"Just acting like you." She plopped down beside me with a thud. "Seriously, what's wrong? You and Sabrina get in a fight?" Okay, maybe she was being empathetic, that is, until she patted my head like a dog.

I sighed, my face sunk into the mattress. "No." I would have preferred a fight with my girlfriend over the horror I had just witnessed.

"Then what?" she sighed dramatically.

"I don't want to talk about it," I mumbled from under my pillow.

"Suit yourself." She got up and slammed the door shut behind her.

My head was dizzy from the image I had seen at the shop. It wasn't just the nudity that would give me nightmares, but seeing Dad with Marnie of all people was the biggest shock. I spent the rest of the night hidden away in my room.

***

The next day I woke before anyone else in the house was up. I snuck out the door and headed for the shop. I could have some quiet time to collect my thoughts. I also retrieved my nearly dead phone, seeing I'd missed numerous texts from Sabrina, and a call from Reggie.

For most of the day, Dad and I had avoided each other; rather, I had avoided him. After two failed attempts to talk to me, and Fletcher asking me out for beers, I managed to escape talking to my dad about him and his lady love.

Unfortunately, I couldn't hide forever. Eventually, we'd have to talk. That night, when I got home from *Lucky's Pub*, I tried to sneak back into my room. I had hidden a burger under my coat, giving Rachel a lame excuse that I had a headache and didn't have much of an appetite. That was partially true- I couldn't stomach my sandwich at lunchtime, thinking about Sophia. I shudder thinking about her, even now! Rachel believed my little white lie about feeling unwell, but someone else didn't.

After I had inhaled my burger, I lay on my bed and closed my eyes. There was a knock at the door. "Go away!" I shouted, thinking that it was Rachel itching to torment me again this evening.

The door creaked open. "Can't you take a hint?" I yelled. I had had enough of her this visit to last me the rest of my life.

"It's me," my dad said. "Can I come in?" he asked as he inched into the room, not waiting for my response.

I rolled over and slammed my head back under my pillow, like an ostrich sticking its head into the sand. Dad was the last person I wanted to talk to.

"I guess."

Dad pulled a rickety wooden chair from my desk and sat down beside me. When I looked up at him, his face was flushed with embarrassment.

"Son," he said, clearing his throat. "Are you okay?"

"Oh, I'm fine, aside from seeing my dad's naked arse!" I shut my eyes to block out the image, but it only made it stand out in my mind.

"Okay, I get that you're upset," he said slowly.

"Why didn't you tell me about Marnie?!" I yelled unexpectedly; the outburst was more from surprise rather than anger. I guess that's what happens when you hold in this frustration.

Dad sank into the chair. "Wyatt, you've always been a bit sensitive when it came to your mother," he said cautiously. "I was afraid that another woman in my life might be more than you were ready for." He scrunched his face.

"Dad, I'm an adult," I said, sitting up on the bed to face him.

"I know." Dad cupped his hands together and added, "But some of those wounds turned into scars that never go away."

I wiped my hands down my face. "I just wish you had told me." I shook my head. "I would've avoided walking in on *that*," I emphasized, referring to the full moon I witnessed last night.

Dad let out a nervous laugh. "Sorry," he raised his shoulders as if to tell me there wasn't anything he could do about that.

"Yeah," I groaned.

"For what it's worth, I'm really happy with Marnie." A grin crept upon his face. "We've been together for six months, not very long."

For most of my childhood, Marnie had been a close family friend. She and Dad spent a lot of time together, and he always insisted they were just friends. "Yeah, right." I jested.

"No, seriously," he smirked. "We've always been friends. But one night after the café was closed, she needed help building some shelves. One thing led to another and..."

I raised my hand. "You can spare me any further details about your private life." I playfully warned him.

"Noted," Dad laughed.

"You'll have to foot the bill for my therapy, but I am happy for you," I offered.

"Okay, okay," he agreed as he got up to leave the room. Just as he was about to go through the doorway, I decided to throw him a curveball.

"Hey, Dad," I asked. Something burned in my mind. "I need to ask you something important."

Dad furrowed his eyebrows, and concern spread across his face. "What's up?"

For years, I had buried any questions I had about Mom's disappearance, but suddenly things were different now. I had just found out about Marnie, and I was contemplating a proposal to Sabrina. I needed some answers.

So, I blurted out, "Why did Mom leave?"

"That's a big one," he admitted. He blew out a long breath as he chose his words.

"Why now?"

"Why not?" I came back.

"Things with Carol, I mean, your mom, were never easy." Dad looked down at the floor. "She had never been thrilled with the idea of marriage. She wanted to travel around Europe and learn how to paint." Dad chuckled. "She had an adventurous soul."

I looked away, and I felt the pain bubbling. Was I ready to hear this?

"When we were in college, she found out that she was pregnant and those dreams of living abroad were squashed." He cleared his throat. "We tried to make it work. We got married. We figured that that was the right thing to do, that everything would fall into place. But it wasn't what Mom wanted."

"Did she resent me and Rachel? Did she prefer her freedom over a family?" I had to ask.

Sensing my upset, Dad said, "Make no mistake, even though her dreams changed, she loved you and your sister very much."

"Then why did she leave us?"

"I think she was unhappy because she felt like I tethered her to Mercer when she wanted to roam freely."

I got up and paced the room.

"She blamed me." My dad rubbed his thighs. "She said that she felt like I suffocated her with family ideals. It had nothing to do with you and your sister." Dad got up and walked over to the window where I was perched. "You two were innocent victims of her unhappiness."

I stared out the window, into the darkness. "Why didn't she at least call us?" That thought had haunted me for years.

Finally, Dad broke the silence and said, "That I don't know, Wyatt. I wish she'd have said something."

"So, then, we'll never know," I replied, choking back some tears. The chapter on my mother was closed. She sure as hell was never coming back. Of that I was certain.

Dad nodded in agreement, patted me on the back, and headed out of my bedroom. Even though he left me on my own to think, he was never very far. I knew he would always be around.

I suppose it's obvious to say that no relationship is perfect. However, it's the imperfections, the cracks, and the flaws that truly define them. My parents' relationship had its struggles, as were Reggie and Betty's. Sabrina and I weren't immune to those moments either; we faced some of our own rough patches, too. Love isn't just about staying when it's easy; it's about choosing to stay when it's difficult.

As I got ready for bed, a memory surfaced. It was of a time when I was sure that Sabrina and I were finished for good. The weight of that eventuality had been unbearable back then, and it still haunts me to this day. I wasn't about to lose her again.

CHAPTER 46

Dana

Tom Chen was my high school sweetheart long before Devin came along. There isn't a single negative thing I could say about Tom, except that he left me heartbroken. We dated for nearly two years when, one day, without warning, he was taken away from me.

I remembered the excitement of falling in love with him. I loved the way his eyes sparkled when he saw me, or the goosebumps I'd get when his fingers grazed mine. The shy smiles, the stolen kisses at our lockers, the notes we'd pass in class filled me with the most innocent of love. Our connection was precious and easy. He was my better half. He had always been proud of my accomplishments, and he was my biggest cheerleader. He even supported me when I memorized a poem about deception and betrayal revolving around a carpenter and a walrus to recite to our English class. Tom was always there for me, even when I was a total geek.

One of the reasons I was sensitive to the holidays was that I lost the love of my life then. If you have any thought that I'm being dramatic, it's because I am. If you've ever met a teenager, drama is a requirement.

The theme of the grade ten winter formal was *Winter Wonderland*. Everyone in high school, by this point, had paired up with someone, for the most part. Wyatt was with Sabrina, Devin was with some girl named Whitney, and Bryan had a date for the formal – even if it was his cousin, Lucy. And I had Tom, or so I thought.

A week before the dance, I remember standing at my locker, organizing what homework I had to take home. "So, what's my Princess wearing for formal?" Tom stuck his head around my locker, startling me. His lips puckered, ready for a kiss.

I kissed his soft pink lips and returned to what I was doing. "I'm not sure, we're headed up north tomorrow to go shopping." I stood up and leaned my head against the locker. I smiled at him, moving closer, until our noses were almost touching.

"Whatever you wear, you'll be the most beautiful girl in the room." As he blinked, I felt the flutter of his dark eyelashes against my skin. He was probably watching one too many teen romance movies, but the words he said were sweet.

The final bell had rung. Tom theatrically broke away from me and started walking away to catch his bus. "Hey!" he called out as he turned around to face me. His grip tightened on the straps of his backpack. "Promise me one thing, Dana." I paused to hear what he had to say: "Always be you, no matter what." I could've sworn everyone around us disappeared. What meaningful message was he trying to send to me?

I looked at him, confused. "What do you mean?" I studied his face for an answer to his riddle.

He stood there, motionless. He stared at me, not answering my question. "I want you to always go after your dreams. Be true to you." He bit his lip, "Promise me." His face grew serious.

I was filled with concern, still not quite understanding what he was trying to say, "I promise." Something didn't feel right, but I couldn't put my finger on it back then.

"Good." And with that, he tore off towards his bus, his destination home.

The weekend seemed off. I heard from Tom less and less. The Thursday before the dance, he plunked himself down beside me in the cafeteria and provided me with some foreshadowing I didn't realize at the time.

"So, my uncle isn't doing well. We might have to go to Toronto this weekend to see him. My mom is worried." He looked down at the table, not meeting my eyes.

I felt disappointment flooding through me. Sensing my sadness, he reached into his pocket and placed a small box on the table in front of me. I eyed it with curiosity, and he nodded at me to open it.

I pulled the lid off and saw a thin silver chain with a rose on it, a little diamond stud in the middle of the flower. "It's not real." Tom was quick to point out his income. "My job at the hardware store doesn't pay enough for the real thing. One day," his eyes shot up to meet mine, hopeful.

I looked down at the gift and smiled. I didn't care if it was real or not. "It's perfect," I mused. I took the necklace out of the box and clasped it around my neck. "How do I look?" I asked my boyfriend.

"Dazzling." He kissed me on the cheek.

The next night, after school, Sabrina came over so we could get ready for the formal. My mom let me buy a white tulle dress with sapphire blue accents. I felt like the Queen of a Winter Ball.

Wyatt picked us up in his dad's truck, and we headed for the school. Tom was going to meet us there. For the first little while, Sabrina, Wyatt and I hung out near the refreshments, as they didn't want to leave me on my own. I wondered, now, if they knew something I didn't about that night. After a while, I encouraged them to go and dance.

There was no point waiting around with me; Tom was coming, wasn't he?

At 9 p.m., I felt a buzzing inside my purse. When I reached in to check my texts, my heart imploded.

Tom: Sorry, we had to leave for Toronto tonight. My uncle is really sick.

I stared down at the message. I felt frozen, unsure of how to respond. Family came first, but what came next, I wasn't prepared for.

I messaged Tom over the weekend, without much reply, asking how his uncle was, and when he was coming back to Mercer. My heart grew weary, but I had to trust that he was coming home.

One week went by. The text messages dwindled. By week two, they were non-existent. What had happened?

The final blow was during science class, fourth period. I'll never forget when Mr. Persaud came into class and struck Tom's name from the attendance list. "Why'd you do that?" I asked him.

Mr. Persaud responded, "Tom doesn't go to this school anymore. He transferred to one in Toronto last week."

I tore out of class and headed into the washroom; I was certain I was going to be sick. I texted Tom one last time.

Dana: How could you?

I never heard from Tom again. He abandoned me for Toronto and took my shattered heart with him.

CHAPTER 47

Reggie

The plan had been set in motion. My letter was with Betty. What better way to win her back than to recreate our wedding day? I'd do anything to see my blushing bride's smile again.

Father Erikson and I had been in touch about the plan to decorate the church. He said it would be all right with him to add a bit more magic to the place. When I asked for some help decorating, he seemed a bit irritated – perhaps I was pushing it to ask him for help. Some people can be so difficult.

Wyatt and I had gone to pick up some extra flower arrangements for the altar from Dana's shop. By the time we got back to the church, Father Erikson and the kids had been busy little elves. The church had been transformed into Bethlehem with a twinkle of Santa Claus for the young kids.

"Where do you want these things, Reggie?" Wyatt asked as he nodded towards a box of leftover holiday items I brought from home. I wanted this to feel as magical as possible.

"How about you hang those things over there?" I pointed to a couple of archways. "I think they'd look nice. Give the room a little extra sparkle." I clasped my hands together.

"Sure. I'll get right to it." Wyatt marched off to get his work done. I knew I could count on him. Wyatt was a good guy, a true friend.

As I surveyed the church, I couldn't help but feel happy with the progress. Things were really coming together. There was still work to be done, but first, there was something I needed to say. I pulled Father Erikson aside to let him in on it. He agreed that it was a good idea to make a clean slate.

I stood near the kids and cleared my throat loudly, or so I thought I did, but no one turned around to look at me. "Excuse me," I tried again, with no acknowledgement. "Excuse me!" I bellowed, and the kids looked around at me, startled.

"Sorry," I muttered, embarrassed. Some of the kids looked afraid. I wanted them to feel relaxed around me; after all, I'm not a bad person, just a grumpy old man. I didn't want these kids to be afraid of me.

"Alright, children." Father Erikson surveyed the room, reluctantly. "Mr. Snow has something he wants to say to all of you." He did a much better job of relaxing the kids than I did.

I took a deep breath and looked at the group of kids. I sure did a number on them when I frightened them, and it was time to make things right.

"Kids, I want to thank you for your help making this space cheerful not only for the holidays, but for the big surprise I have in store for my wife, Betty." I wrung my hands for what came next. "I have been thinking long and hard about my recent behaviour. I wanted to say how sorry I was for misbehaving when you came to sing at my home." As I paused, I couldn't help but notice the multiple sets of eyes darting at each other as if to seek confirmation that I was apologizing for being a grump. "I want to say how sorry I am for not being appreciative of your singing. I know you've worked hard. And I want to apologize for the snow falling on you when I slammed the door."

One of the kids, wide-eyed, leaned towards Father Erikson, and I heard him say, "Is Mr. Snow *for real*?"

"My boy, yes, he is." Father Erikson shrugged and returned my gaze.

When no one said anything, I felt embarrassed. Did my apology not matter?

"Anyways, thanks again. I think this will be a very special surprise for my wife. And, as a token of my appreciation, Miss Marnie made us a special batch of peppermint brownies and hot chocolate to have when we're finished here."

My apology was met with an unenthusiastic reply. I did what I needed to do; my conscience was clear, for now. Before I had a chance to help Wyatt, one of the little girls came up to me and asked, "Aren't you already married to Mrs. Snow?"

"I am," I kneeled to meet the pint-sized kid at eye level. "She's a very special lady." I smiled, thinking back to the vows we made on our wedding day.

"Can you marry the same person more than once?" She asked, puzzled.

"You can marry the person you love as many times as you'd like. If I could, I'd marry her every single day; she's that special to me." I rubbed my cheek, trying to brush away small tears that had trickled down my face. I didn't want the little girl to see me cry.

The little girl thought carefully, processing what I said. "I love Jared," she looked over her shoulder and pointed to a little boy in a blue plaid shirt. "Maybe I can marry him, too."

I couldn't help but grin. "Maybe," I wiggled my eyebrows at her. She tore off towards her crush and wrapped her arms around his tiny frame. I could have sworn that his eyes bulged out of his head when she launched herself at him.

I looked over at Wyatt as he hung twinkle lights over the archway. He reminded me of myself at that age, full of love and hope for the future. I sure hope he and Sabrina end up together. They made a good couple. I think there is hope for all of us lonely hearts.

CHAPTER 48

WYATT

One of my biggest regrets in life was losing Sabrina. No, it wasn't from the dreaded turkey dump, a job in a city, or waiting too long to propose; no, the breakup happened in high school, when Tom Chen left Dana and moved to Toronto.

Teenage love can be very dramatic—no, I'm not talking about those two historical teenage lovebirds who died in the name of love, or the one who offered his love interest the floating wooden door and sank to the bottom of the Atlantic Ocean. Teenage love can make you feel like you can't eat or sleep, listening to breakup songs on repeat until you feel all your emotions.

Dana had found out from Mr. Persaud that Tom had left for Toronto without talking to her. She had to find out from her teacher, of all people, that he'd changed schools. Tom had a lot of nerve to do that to her; they were so in love!

For weeks, Dana was in a slump. She wouldn't come to school, so Sabrina took her homework and updated her on the assignments. The teachers were cool about it for the first week, but when the heartbreak droned on for three more weeks, the empathy wore off, and Dana's parents got phone calls about her truancies.

"I just don't get it," Dana sniffled between words. "Why would he leave me?" Sabrina passed Dana facial tissues until the box was empty. Most evenings, Sabrina and I would pop by Dana's house for a little while, trying to coax her out into civilization again; most of the time, our efforts were fruitless, but occasionally she surprised us, and she'd walk with us to the convenience store to get soda and sour candies.

"I don't know," Sabrina and I said in unison. We repeated this sentence a hundred times. Dana would constantly try to dissect every interaction leading up to Tom's leaving. My head spun from all of the different conspiracy theories.

"It sucks," I tried to offer. I could empathize, to a point. When my mom up and left, my brain was full of similar thoughts. You can't make sense of other people's behaviour – it is what it is, and sometimes it may not make sense to you, but it makes sense to the person who left.

"Totally sucks," Sabrina nodded. We had prodded Dana out of bed and made our way down the slushy street for treats. Dana was still fashioning her fuzzy purple pyjamas. We had wrapped her in her dad's winter coat before she had a chance to argue with us. "He's such a jerk," Sabrina sighed.

As we walked, for some reason, my thoughts shifted. "You know, he probably wanted to talk to you. Maybe there was too much going on with his uncle," I trailed off as Sabrina and Dana craned their necks to look at me.

With her mouth gaping open, she finally said, "As if you'd justify that," Sabrina turned on me.

I paused on the sidewalk to look at her, "I mean, family first. Right?" If only my mom thought that.

I could see the anger raging in her eyes. "Don't you see what this has done to Dana?" She pulled our friend in closer. "I hardly think standing up for Tom is the best move. Do you?" She scowled at me. Dana stood there, numb, stuck in the crossfire.

I puffed out hot air, "I just mean, his parents decided to leave Mercer, not him." I was inching into dangerous territory, but maybe Tom deserved defending; needless to say, I felt conflicted.

Sabrina started to drag Dana down the sidewalk. "Well, why don't you just call him up and ask?" Sabrina's words stabbed me.

"Hey, why are you fighting?" Dana sniffled, "I think enough has happened recently; let's cool it." We got to the convenience store, and Dana headed inside. Sabrina tugged at the sleeve of my coat and stalled outside to hash things out.

In a low, whispered voice, she said, "What was that?" A scowl crossed her face.

"What?" I asked sheepishly. I was friends with Tom, too. I hadn't heard from the guy since he left. He had ghosted everyone. I believed, though, that he needed time to think things over.

"That?" She pointed to the recent past. "Why were you defending Tom?" She crossed her arms. I knew that I was in trouble.

I shifted my weight and my options. "I think there's more to the story than we know." Was I not allowed to defend him? Did I have to take a side?

"What about Dana?" Sabrina cried.

"What about her?" I threw my hands up in the air.

"She's our friend! Don't you want to protect her?" The edges of her chapped lips trembled. I didn't understand why Sabrina was escalating over this.

"Don't you think it's time she moved on?" I tried to reason, but in retrospect, maybe it was too soon to try to reason Tom's behaviours as well as Dana's choice on how she was handling the situation.

Sabrina practically yelled, "Wyatt! I can't believe you right now!"

I decided to throw a curveball, to see if the conversation would change, and boy, did it ever. "Hey, maybe their love wasn't supposed to last. Maybe they're just seasons."

Sabrina hissed at me. "Maybe *we're* just seasons." Those words sure did come back to bite me in the ass.

"What's that supposed to mean?" I panicked. Was Sabrina breaking up with me?

The conversation paused, and so did my furiously beating heart. "Maybe we need to take a break."

Ouch. "Why?" She could not be serious right now. "What did I do?"

"You don't believe in love."

What a stone-cold thing to say! Of course, I believed in love! Sure, those thoughts have been challenged at times, but I believed in love, especially with her!

"I do! Why would you say that?" I couldn't believe what I was hearing. Was this the end of us?

Dana popped her head outside. "Are you guys okay?" She asked, reluctantly. "I need help with the slushy machine." Dana never quite got the hang of that rickety old thing.

Sabrina's nose was glowing red. "Yeah, we'll be in shortly." She forced a smile. Dana headed back inside to continue her candy consumption.

I moved in towards her. "Seriously, Sabrina, what are you doing?"

"If you can't support Dana with her love life, then I guess you don't support ours."

Love life? More like a love lie. "The two things have nothing to do with each other." I contended.

Sabrina looked down at her feet. "I think we need to take a break, figure things out."

"What?" I wailed.

"Maybe we'll go our separate ways once we graduate," Sabrina said matter-of-factly. She was tearing my heart apart.

"That's not what I want, Sabrina!" Was this the end of our relationship?

"Maybe that's what you need, a wake-up call to figure shit out." With that, Sabrina went inside and left me out in the cold.

What had just happened?

***

I never totally understood why Sabrina ditched me; it was a silly fight, after all. You could argue that we were broken up, or like the famous sitcom couple – maybe we were on a break.

For two weeks, Sabrina didn't call or return my text messages. She didn't sit beside me on the bus or eat with me at lunch. She'd vanish into thin air every time I tried to walk towards her when we were in the crowded hallways at school. Sabrina didn't want anything to do with me; perhaps this was the end.

Eventually, Dana came back to school, still in a daze; I don't think she entirely noticed that Sabrina and I weren't talking, as she still seemed preoccupied with thoughts of Tom. Eventually, Devin started lurking around her locker, but Dana didn't pay much attention to him until the following year.

One day, in chemistry class, we had to pair up for an assignment. Mrs. Simons had given us our project instructions. All my classmates started to buzz, asking who wanted to buddy up with them. I looked around the room to see if Sabrina would make eye contact with me. We were usually partners. Since Tom had left, Sabrina picked Dana to partner up with instead. I was left alone; I was beginning to think that this would be the new normal – Sabrina didn't want anything to do with me.

"Need a partner?" A nasally voice asked.

I looked up to see Tamara Adams staring down at me, her length of curls draped around her shoulders. Tamara wasn't exactly studious, but there didn't seem to be anyone else left. "Looks like you're on your own," she said as she studied her manicured nails.

"Sure," I said cautiously, looking back to see if Sabrina had noticed. "I need a partner."

"Awesome," She plunked down beside me, eying me from the side. I had an inkling that Tamara had more in mind than just a chemistry experiment, but I wasn't willing to give up on Sabrina just yet, even if Tamara was openly flirting with me.

For a week, Tamara and I worked on our experiment. She'd laugh at all my jokes, even when they weren't particularly funny. She'd say, "Wyatt, stop!" as she playfully slapped my arm. There were a couple of times I saw her look back at Sabrina, and she'd become even more handsy with me. Maybe she was trying to make Sabrina jealous. I didn't mind, I wanted to see if it elicited a response from my former flame.

At the end of the week, as we were packing up, Tamara dropped her textbook on the floor. "Opps." She giggled. "I'm so clumsy!" She didn't make any attempt to bend over to pick up her books.

I looked down at the mess. It wasn't going to pick itself up. "Here, let me help you," I leaned down to pick up the book.

"What a gentleman," she gushed, as she twisted her hair around her fingertip. I swear I saw her wink at me. My face flushed.

"No problem," I smiled.

I saw Sabrina exit the classroom and I longed to talk to her, but maybe I should try to forget her and move on.

"I was thinking," Tamara scooped her books up in her arms, "Maybe we could go to the movies this weekend." She batted her thick eyelashes. "There's a new slasher movie I'd *love* to see."

Oh no, that sounded like a date. Not just a movie, but one she'd probably want me to put my arm around her for. I wasn't sure what to do. Sabrina wasn't exactly talking to me, but I just wasn't ready to give up on her either.

I could feel my palms beginning to sweat. "Uh," I stalled.

"Sorry, Wyatt's busy this weekend," someone interjected.

"Oh," Tamara eyed Sabrina up and down, "I didn't know you two were still *a thing*." She emphasized.

"We are," her tone sharp, "you can forget about my boyfriend," she challenged Tamara.

"Okay," Tamara raised her eyebrows, and clucked her tongue. "I'll see you Monday, Wyatt. Unless you want to study at my house this weekend," Tamara couldn't resist taking a jab at Sabrina one more time.

"Like I said, he's busy," Sabrina fired back with daggers in her eyes.

After Tamara walked away, Sabrina turned to me. "Were you really going to go out with her?" I sensed some panic in her voice.

"No, I don't know – maybe?" I really wasn't sure what to say.

"You like her?" Sabrina asked. It sounded as if she didn't really want to know the answer.

"No, I like you," I tried to reassure her, "but you were a little MIA these past couple of weeks." I zipped up my backpack and hoisted it over my shoulder.

"I know," She bit her lip. "I'm sorry."

"No need to be sorry," I muttered. I wasn't someone who liked confrontation.

"I didn't want her to stick her talons into you." Her lips turned up in a curl.

I couldn't help but laugh. Sabrina always had a wicked sense of humour. "Is she a bird of prey?" I folded my arms across my chest.

"Yes," Sabrina hip-checked me. "And you're her victim, romantic roadkill." She started to laugh uncontrollably.

"What an image." I broke out in laughter, too.

After a few minutes of silliness, we stopped and took a more serious turn. "Anyway, I do owe you an apology about Tom." Sabrina reached for my hand.

"Seriously, let's just forget it. I mean it." I squeezed her fingers between mine.

"Yes, I do. I shouldn't have gotten upset with you about your friend." She brushed her hair behind her ear with her free hand. "You're allowed to have an opinion."

"I am?" I asked in a mock-shocked tone.

"Don't push it," she laughed.

"Tom's leaving was a shock, and yeah, he could've handled it better – but he didn't." We headed out into the hallway. "We may never know what actually happened."

When we got to Sabrina's locker, she fiddled with the metal combination lock, wrenched the old door open and dumped her books inside. "I know. I worry."

"Why?" I propped my arm on the top of the locker door.

"What if love doesn't last?" Sabrina caught her sad gaze in the locker mirror.

"Ours will," I tried to break her trance and make eye contact with her.

She turned to look at me. "How do you know?"

"I just do." I shrugged. "Have faith."

"Do you have a crystal ball?" Sabrina chided.

"No, but I think Marnie might." Which was possible; she was into the woo-woo magic stuff. I'd have to ask her next time I pop down to the café.

"Be serious."

"I think we just have to live in the moment," I kissed her, "and hope for the best."

Sabrina leaned into me for another kiss. "That sounds like a plan to me." For the first time in weeks, we held hands as we walked to our next class together.

And just like that, Sabrina and I were back together. No more worry, no more heartache. It was a close call, back then. But she was right, love might not last – but that shouldn't stop you from enjoying it when you have it.

CHAPTER 49

Dana

Tom Chen. Of course, it was him! The mystery was solved. There were no other broken hearts to be accounted for.

But why did he wait until now to come back to Mercer? Why did he wait to get in touch with me? It's been almost a decade.

"Your high school sweetheart?" Marnie asked, confused, as she set up her hot chocolate stand at the Mercer Christmas Eve Market. "I thought Devin was your high school sweetheart?"

I took a large peppermint brownie and shoved it into my mouth. "Devin came after Tom." I chewed, trying to swallow the large hunk of baked goodies, and my feelings. "Devin was more of a distraction." I swallowed hard, worried that I would face yet another ghost from my romantic past.

Marnie nodded as she dumped rainbow-coloured marshmallows into a bowl. I reached down and took a handful of the fluffy goodness. As I went in for another handful, she slapped my hand away. "Those are for *paying* customers," she emphasized. Her gold rings seemed to dance in the twilight.

"I'm eating my feelings!" I cried out. Didn't she understand that this was a crisis?

Marnie grabbed hold of my shoulders and gave me a gentle shake. "Get a hold of yourself, woman!" She smiled as she playfully slapped my shoulder.

"I can't! I can't!" I wailed. My emotions were bubbling over. I was no longer in control of what would happen next. "I think I'm going to be sick!" The reeling of my stomach overtook my thoughts.

Marnie looked at me with playful annoyance. "I can see that." She set down the shaker of chocolate sprinkles and grabbed my hands. "What will be, will be." I took comfort in the soft caressing of her fingers. "How exciting is it that your high school love wants to rekindle your romance!" Marnie pulled me in for a celebratory hug, although I didn't feel like celebrating anything. The mystery still wasn't quite solved.

I looked past her and scowled. "What if I don't want him back? He abandoned me!"

She looked at me with sad eyes. "It doesn't sound like he had much of a choice from what you shared. He was only a kid."

"Don't defend him!" I pulled away from her. I wrapped my weary arms around myself.

"I'm not, I'm just trying to see things from his perspective." Marnie gave me a sympathetic look. "I want you to be happy."

Deep down inside, I wanted to be happy too, even if pieces of old hurt rose to the surface.

As the late afternoon droned on, more and more vendors set up shop inside and outside of the legion, getting ready for the last-minute shoppers. I finished setting up my table, and Wyatt had finished setting up the photobooth to take pictures of lovers kissing underneath the mistletoe.

"So, do you know what you'll say to him tonight?" Wyatt chimed in on the detective work. How was he so confident that he knew who the sender of the letters was?

Sabrina elbowed him in the ribs. "We don't even know if it's him," she winked. She wanted to see for herself who the suspect was.

"Well, who else could it be? He's the obvious choice." Wyatt was oblivious to the research that Sabrina and I had already invested in.

We looked at each other, shocked. "He is?" Sabrina and I said in unison. Wyatt could *not* be serious right now. If he knew it was Tom, why didn't he say anything sooner?

Wyatt laughed and said, "Yeah, of course! Tom was your first true love." Wyatt looked at us as if we were both failing to use our common sense. Maybe we should've let Wyatt in on our reindeer games.

A small smile spread across my face because deep down, I knew that he was right. I had a few other loves along the way, but Tom was the first person I truly loved.

CHAPTER 50

Reggie

The waiting game had begun.

I'm an impatient man, so you can imagine how agonizing waiting was for me. I needed a distraction, something positive to focus on. Every time I tried to refocus my thoughts, I found myself thinking about rejection.

What if Betty said no to me? What if Betty has left me for good? What if Betty has found another man?

I slammed my fist onto the recliner, giving myself a jolt. "Get a hold of yourself, Reggie. You can't think like that!" I shouted out loud. And that was the truth. I couldn't think like that. And so, I decided to call the one person who could give me the support that I needed; I needed a good pep talk to snap myself out of this funk.

My clumsy fingers picked up the dreaded cellphone. I fumbled with the flat screen until the numbers illuminated the tiny electronic rectangle.

"Hey, Dad," my only child said when she answered the phone. "How are you?"

"I'm holding up," I tried to be as cheery as possible. I needed to hold onto some shred of optimism.

"Are you?" she asked.

"Yes, you little worrywart," I teased her. "I have a lot to fill you in on." For the next half hour, I told Maggie about my grand attempt to win back her mother. She gasped with delight as I told her what me, and my friends, were getting up to.

"Well, Dad. It sounds marvellous! You've been working hard, and it's showing." I could almost hear her smile into the phone.

"Thanks, honey." I exhaled a deep breath, "I'm anxious but looking forward to the big day."

"Any plans for Christmas?" She asked nervously. I knew she was worried about my being alone for the holidays. This would be the first time, in a long time, that I'd be alone at this time of year.

"No," I sighed. "Bruce and I will check out the Christmas Day football game. Perhaps he and I will indulge in a little daytime spiked eggnog." I smiled as the furball lifted his head. "Yes, I'm talking about you, Bruce." I patted his backside.

"Dad! You can't give the cat eggnog! That'll make him sick!"

"Cats like milk!" I defended myself, "Can't a man share some holiday spirit with his cat?" I laughed.

"Not spiked milk. You're a bit of a misfit, aren't you?" She groaned.

"Guilty as charged."

"Okay, Dad. I'm sorry, but I have to let you go. I've got to get up early tomorrow for work." She sounded sad and exhausted. I guess shift work will do that to you.

I hated saying goodbye, but I didn't want her to be tired tomorrow because of me.

"Okay, honey. I love you." My heart sank; I didn't want to hang up.

"I love you, too, Dad."

As soon as Maggie hung up the phone, I decided that I had one last thing to do to make my plan complete. I got out the phonebook, yes, they still make those and found the number I was searching for. After a few rings, I heard a familiar voice on the other end of the receiver.

"*Holiday Travel*, Martha speaking. How may I help you?" Martha sang into the phone.

"Martha!" I said as I matched her enthusiasm. "It's Reggie Snow." I cleared my throat, "I was wondering if you could do me a favour," If Betty were here, she'd remind me of my manners, "please." Yes, my plan was falling perfectly into place. There was one final piece of the puzzle, but that move was up to my wife.

CHAPTER 51

Wyatt

I had fulfilled my due diligence by completing last-minute work orders at the shop, assisting Reggie with decorating the church, and repairing some flickering lights at the photobooth. I decided that I deserved a break.

I wandered among the vendors, looking at the goods. I still wanted to get Sabrina something special for Christmas. I had already picked up one small item for her, but it would look rather lonely all by itself under the large tree Rachel insisted we get. Rachel always had an obsession with decorating the perfect Christmas tree, as if that made up for our mom walking out on us all those years ago.

I should have paid more attention to my surroundings; if I had, I would have turned on my heels when I saw her.

"Hey, Wy," Marnie said nervously. "How are you?" She was trying to make amends with me. It was quite the shock to discover that she and my dad were an item. I couldn't help but feel a bit betrayed by both of them. Things were awkward now, sure, but I'm sure it won't always be this way.

I forced a smile. She was the last person that I wanted to talk to. Not that I was mad at her, per se, but rather that she and my dad had kept this secret from me and Rachel for so long.

She wrung her hands together. "Could we talk?" she cut to the chase. Marnie was not usually one to sugarcoat things.

As much as I didn't want to have this conversation, particularly since I felt I had smoothed things over with my dad, I knew it was necessary. "Sure," I shoved my shivering hands into my coat pocket.

"First of all, I'm sorry you witnessed that in the shop," she looked away, "it's hard for us to get alone time, especially since your sister came home."

I wanted to barf. I didn't want to think about what bedroom shenanigans my dad and Marnie got up to. There are some things a kid doesn't need to know, regardless of how old they are.

I waved a hand, brushing her off. I didn't need to hear any more. "It's fine," my eyes fluttered, avoiding contact. Sabrina hated it when I was conflict avoidant.

Marnie let out a sigh, "No, it's not fine," she rearranged some bowls of marshmallows and chocolate sprinkles shakers in her booth, knowing she'd probably already arranged her setup perfectly. We all had our odd little habits when we're nervous. "We should have told you we were a couple a long time ago." As much as I wished they had, I could appreciate why they didn't come out and say anything to us, they wanted their privacy.

Curiosity got the best of me. "Why didn't you?" I wanted to know why I was kept in the dark for so long.

"We knew it might be hard, given Carol, I mean your mom, leaving." She clasped her hands together, giving me sad eyes – the same sad eyes people gave me when our mom left. "We knew it was hard for you and your sister. We didn't want to add to the hurt."

"I'm an adult," I reminded her. "Mom left a long time ago." I wasn't a little kid who needed protecting.

"That you are, but you are still Lou's son. You always have, and you always will be." Marnie brushed her hair behind her ear. "He's protective of you."

"I just wish I knew." I ran my hand down my face.

Marnie popped a marshmallow in her mouth. "I know. I'm sorry," she chewed nervously. I don't think I've ever seen Marnie shaken up before. I suppose she genuinely felt bad.

"You don't need to apologize," I reassured her.

"I owe it to you." She made a cup of hot chocolate, topped with whipped cream and sprinkles, and passed it to me.

"I've always wanted my dad to be happy. I was worried that he was lonely." I looked Marnie in the eyes. There was no need to be embarrassed anymore. "I'm glad he found happiness with you." I opened my arms wide to embrace her. "You're a catch," I whispered in her ear.

"Finally, you caught on!" she giggled, squeezing me back.

Like the little ninja she was, Rachel sauntered up to the booth. "Hey, Marnie! Are you coming over for Christmas dinner tomorrow night?"

Marnie cast me a look, "If that's okay with everyone else, I'm free."

"You're welcome to come." I extended my olive branch.

"Thanks, Wy." Marnie squeezed my shoulder, then turned to tend to her customers.

Rachel and I walked away. "Hey, did you know about Dad and Marnie?" I asked my annoying little sister.

"Yeah, loser." She grabbed my drink and took a sip of my hot chocolate. "Where have you been?" She perused the next booth. "Don't you see how they look at each other?"

"Shut up," I bumped into Rachel, trying to knock her over. It wasn't easy for her, trying to trudge through the snow in her 6-inch-heeled boots. She was walking in the streets of Mercer, not some Paris runway.

"No, *you* shut up." Rachel shoved me back. Some things never change.

"Hey guys!" Bryan waved at us.

"Oh no," Rachel panicked. "Let's get out of here!" She pulled my arm, trying to lead me deeper into the crowd. I pulled back and headed towards Bryan.

"No, we can't be rude. It's Christmas!" I shoved Rachel towards Bryan, turned and headed in another direction. I needed to throw Rachel to the wolves so I could finish what I needed to do. Sabrina was in for the best night of her life, and I didn't need Rachel meddling *again*.

CHAPTER 52

Dana

At 7 p.m., the customers were in full swing; the legion was packed with last-minute shoppers. Child carolers, led by Father Erikson, sang holiday classics as the snow drifted down on the market. Their parents looked on with beaming faces as they snapped photos of their kids. People were buying gifts left, right, and center; the vendors would make great transactions tonight. Even the animal shelter was enjoying generous sales of their holiday calendars as well as receiving sizable charitable donations. Everyone was in a giving spirit, just in time for the holidays.

I was so lost in the hustle and bustle of the market while I packed mistletoe in simple, brown paper bags that I completely forgot about the letters and their mysterious sender. Finally, I felt a moment of freedom to experience the holiday joy. It was heartening to see everyone so happy and in the holiday spirit. As soon as my table was cleared, I would be free to join the others. I hoped Marnie had some brownies left; I had more feelings to eat.

"Got any of those mistletoe things left?" a familiar voice asked. When I turned around, Mr. Snow was standing at my booth. My favourite customer had come to purchase a last minute gift for his wife.

"For you, I certainly do." I took one of the last few bundles on the table and wrapped it in gold tissue paper, being careful not to damage the delicate leaves. I was certain that he was adding this to the romantic surprise he was planning for his wife. She's such a lucky lady. I couldn't imagine being married that long to someone. I took a moment to ponder. Maybe I did want someone to love after all, someone to laugh and to bicker with. Damn, they were lucky to be in love.

As I went to hand Mr. Snow his parcel, I couldn't help but see a tear form in the corner of his eye. "Are you alright?" I asked.

He took a moment to collect himself as he bit his bottom lip. "Yes, just reminiscing." He took in a deep breath and let out a slow, long sigh. It felt as if he was releasing an avalanche of emotions.

"The holidays do that, don't they?" I said as he finally took the parcel from my gloved hand and held on tightly to the paper handles.

"They sure do." He cleared his throat, "I- we hope to join Maggie in the city for New Year's Day. She's busy working the holiday this year." It was unfortunate his daughter had to work over the holiday; that's part of the job as a nurse, I supposed.

I tried to lift his mood, but it was clear that something was bothering him. "Well, I hope tomorrow isn't too quiet for you. I'm sure there's a football game on."

A weary smile crossed his lips. "I've got Bruce to keep me company." Mr. Snow began to walk away; his frown resembled a melting snowman.

I gave Mr. Snow a puzzled look. "And Betty, too," I added. Things were slowly starting to add up.

"Of course," Mr. Snow awkwardly chuckled, "Betty, too." His face reddened from embarrassment for his omission. He took a few more shuffled steps in the snow. "Merry Christmas, Dana."

"Merry Christmas to you, too." I began to worry about my favourite customer. I hoped he was alright. I couldn't help but fret; was something amiss in the Snow household?

CHAPTER 53

Reggie

Is it at all possible that I will be spending my first Christmas alone? It's beginning to look that way. Maybe the bachelor's life is in my future, but I hoped not. I made my way home in the freshly fallen snow—time to relax and settle in for the night, with Bruce and a beer.

When I opened the front door, I was greeted by the ever-faithful feline. He was my friendliest of companions. I didn't deserve him. I hoped that, if Betty had left me for good, she wouldn't take her cat with her. I made a fire, took a beer out of the fridge, and settled into my recliner. Bruce hopped into my lap and promptly fell asleep, and for once, I didn't mind his intrusion into my personal space.

For what it was worth, going into town and spending time with the people of Mercer, some of whom I consider friends, even loosely, warmed my heart. Everyone was in the holiday spirit, even me, thanks to Father Erikson. I loved seeing everyone come together to have a town-inspired celebration. There were a few last-minute shoppers like Bryan trying to get a few extra gifts to put under the tree. I wasn't bothered by people like that annoying Bob Collins kissing his wife! Even the kid carolers sounded a lot better. Maybe they had been practising.

I sat in quiet contemplation. While surrounded by ghosts of Christmas past, family ornaments on the tree and wedding-inspired Christmas photos. I felt somewhat at peace. Whatever would be, would be. I had come to accept that.

A commotion outside, most likely caused by the neighbours welcoming their holiday guests, caused Bruce to stir. I petted his silky fur as he opened his sleepy eyes. "I got you something, you little menace," I said, reaching down beside me into a shopping bag. I took out a knitted mouse, filled with catnip, and handed it to him. He sniffed it, and his eyes opened wide. I couldn't help but laugh.

I chucked the toy onto the floor and watched as Bruce batted it with expert precision. Then, he clutched it with his paws, nails outstretched, like the jungle animal he was descended from. That would keep him occupied for a while. Cats were such interesting creatures. At least he was enjoying himself. I desperately wanted to make someone happy this holiday, even if it wasn't the love of my life.

The quiet of the evening was interrupted by the rattling of the rear door's handle. My heart almost stopped. An intruder? On Christmas Eve? Nervously, I rose from my chair and inched cautiously towards the rear of the house.

Any thought that the noise might be made by Betty returning was dashed when a familiar voice called out, "I'm home!"

"Maggie, what are you doing here?" I asked with a mile-wide smile stretching across my face. "I thought you had to work?"

"I traded with someone who owed me a favour. I didn't want you to be alone on Christmas," she whispered in my ear as she held me tight.

I pulled back from our embrace, looked her in the eyes, and mouthed "thank you." I couldn't resist pulling her in again for another long hug. Perhaps this holiday wasn't going to be so bad after all, I had the other half of my heart with me.

CHAPTER 54

Wyatt

Everything around us looked perfect: freshly fallen snow laced the green shrubbery, festive lights adorned the vendor's huts, and the stars above twinkled, adding a special nostalgic glow. I felt as if I was in a snow globe or the winter wonderland Dana had set up in her shop.

The entire evening felt surreal. Everything had fallen into place. I intentionally set up the photobooth to create the perfect background for a proposal. When the lines eventually cleared, I would take Sabrina's hand and, under the mistletoe, ask her the big question, the most important question I've ever asked anyone in my entire life.

As the moment neared my stomach was in knots. I was having difficulty forming words, but I was determined to say what was in my heart.

I couldn't help but admire Sabrina tonight. I watched her from a distance as she spoke to my dad and sister. I loved that they got along so well. She fit perfectly into my family. My heart was full as I watched her laugh along with my loved ones. I adored it when she threw her head back and let out a cackle. Her smile lit up my heart and calmed my nerves.

I crashed back to reality when someone rammed into me. "Sorry, Wyatt!" Todd Thompson apologized after he knocked me to the ground. "I wasn't paying attention." That kid should try out for high school football; he'd make the team for sure.

My pulse was quick; I was anxious enough right now. "All good, Merry Christmas." I waved to him as I brushed snow off my pant legs.

"You, too. Wyatt!" Todd scuttled off with his friends.

I tapped my pocket to make certain that the small, rectangular box was still there. I breathed a sigh of relief when I felt it stashed safely in my coat, right up tight against my heart.

Just like Reggie, I had a plan in place. It was almost time to get down on bended knee. I knew she was the one. It had taken me a while to realize that and to make sure our forever had been mapped out. I had second guessed myself for so long over my parents' past that I forgot to live, to follow my heart. I know now that that's what mattered the most.

I was ready. I was confident. Sabrina would say 'yes' when I asked her to marry me. Just as I was about to approach my future bride, I saw him - Dana's secret admirer finally showed up. He was coming to claim his soulmate, just as I was about to propose to mine.

CHAPTER 55

Dana

With the final piece of mistletoe sold, I took the opportunity to check out the other vendors in the market. Before long, I had an arm full of parcels: sweets for my parents, a stained-glass ornament for Sabrina, and homemade dog treats for Ruby. My holiday shopping was finally completed. I returned to my booth to tuck my parcels under the table until it was time to go home.

It was just then that I felt a familiar presence. I can't quite explain it, but you know the feeling, the one where you can sense that you're being watched?

Then, a voice, that voice, from the past broke the silence. When I turned around, there he was, looking longingly at me. The space between us seemed to close.

"I wish I had never left," he confessed. "I wish we had stayed together." He moved slowly towards me. I felt as if everyone else around us had disappeared.

I didn't know whether to laugh or to cry. It was him. "Tom," I barely pushed his name past my lips. My chest filled with love. Tears streamed down my face. "Is it you?" I was in high school again, at our lockers, sharing butterfly kisses before the final bell rang.

His eyes locked on mine as a smile tugged at the corners of his mouth. "Were you expecting someone else?" he asked, as the smile overtook his entire face. "I'm in town visiting my parents for Christmas. They moved back a few months ago." He laced his gloved fingers together. "The city wasn't for them."

Even though my heart was filled with love for him, I couldn't let go of the pain he caused me so many years ago. There were so many 'whys' that I needed answers to. Instinctively, he could see and feel all of the emotions that must have been expressed on my face and in my eyes.

"I didn't have a choice when we moved away." He took a step toward me. "My mom needed to take care of my uncle." With each word that he spoke, the gap between us began to narrow. "I was heartbroken. I was ashamed of how we left. I couldn't face you." He ran his hands through his hair. "There was a lot of pressure in my family at the time; I didn't have a say."

"You broke my heart," I said, my voice trembling under the weight of the words. The hurt boiled inside me, raw and unrelenting, threatening to spill over, my chest tightening with the urge to scream, to let the pain consume the silence between us. But instead, I stood there, every ounce of my being caught between anger and longing.

He shoved his hands deep into the pockets of his forest green bomber jacket, his shoulders slumping under the weight of words he could barely say. "I know," he whispered, his voice barely audible. After a moment, he looked up and added, "I'm sorry."

I believed him. When Tom spoke, there was no trace of the boy who had once broken my heart—only a man carrying regrets. Marnie had been right. He *was* just a kid back then, trapped in circumstances far bigger than either of us. I couldn't imagine the weight his family bore, the sacrifices they made to care for his sick uncle. In retrospect, he could have said something, anything, instead of just disappearing.

But we don't get to rewrite history. Mistakes linger in the cracks of who we are, shaping us, but never letting us go back. All we can do is move forward.

"I'm sorry, too," I said, the words gentle, like a balm over an old scar. Around us, the crowd moved without care, oblivious to the fragile connection being rebuilt in their midst. The ache of the past had softened, and for the first time, I felt as if an old wound had truly healed.

He smiled. "You seem to be doing okay for yourself." Damn his smile. It was melting my cold, cold heart.

"I have a collection of newspaper clippings in my desk drawer. I've been following your success story in the Mercer paper. You've made quite a name for yourself."

Unable to contain my pride, I blushed. For a moment, my guard was broken by Tom's compliments, but I quickly regained my composure and pressed the issue. "Why did you send me the letters?" I asked. He could have been more direct.

"I didn't know how you would react if I just showed up out of the blue. I had to be sure that I wasn't making another mistake, that you still had feelings for me." Tom moved closer to me, closing both the lapsed time and distance. "I want you. My life is empty without the woman I love."

"*Loved*," I corrected him. I adjusted my toque as I let my comment sear his heart.

"I never once stopped loving you." He studied me for a moment, "Did you ever stop loving me?" I sensed his concern that our renewed connection might now be lost.

I winced. My emotional armour was slipping, but I still needed to protect my heart.

A worried look crossed his face. "Tell me you don't love me anymore, and I'll leave," he bit his bottom lip in anticipation of my answer.

I tried hard to search for the right words. I wanted to be upset at him for leaving, but I longed for him. My emotions were all over the place, but I had to follow my heart.

"Dana, will you consider giving me another chance?" he offered me his hand.

Before he had a chance to say another word, I kissed him. It was a kiss to make up for lost time. Our public embrace was met with hoots and hollers, and shouts of "Get a room!"

When we finally untethered ourselves, we walked over to the photobooth to solidify this holiday reunion with a documented kiss. After Tom and Wyatt shared a manly reunion hug, we embraced under my handmade mistletoe while Wyatt counted down to the flash. Once more Tom's lips were on mine and would be for many Christmases to come. Of that I was certain.

"You know, those letters freaked me out." I teased him.

He pulled back to look me in the eyes, "What? You used to love puzzles when we were kids," his mouth wide open in fake shock.

"Yeah, for crosswords! I thought I had a stalker!" I said as I smacked his shoulder.

It was as if nothing had changed between us, despite the passage of time, except that maturity had given us both a new perspective. Tom was back, and he saw me for me; he loved me for me. And I loved him. This was a second chance for both of us, an opportunity not to be missed.

And with that realization, I kissed my second chance at love one last time under the mistletoe and continued to kiss him until right before the clock struck midnight, signalling the start of Christmas Day.

It's true what they say: sometimes love comes around once in a lifetime, and sometimes it comes around a second time when you meet someone special under the mistletoe.

CHAPTER 56

Reggie

Christmas had came and went. Maggie had to leave early this morning for her night shift, but, before she left, she reassured me that everything was going to be fine and then pulled out of the driveway and headed back to the city.

I spent most of the morning debating what to wear on Boxing Day, and then the rest of the afternoon agonizing over the decorations at the church. I paced so much that Father Erikson said that I was going to wear a hole in the floor.

Late afternoon transitioned into evening. I felt as if my prospects were waning. "She probably isn't coming," I whispered to myself. I was deflated. I checked the breast pocket of my navy suit jacket. Inside was the folded photo of my wife on our wedding day, those many years ago. I was reassured that the picture was still there, even if she wasn't. That picture has, and always will, last me a lifetime. I wish I had taken better care of it.

Planning a surprise like this was a risk. I felt somewhat foolish. Maybe Betty wouldn't want to renew our vows. She certainly hadn't responded positively to my other grand gestures of love. What was going to make this any different?

I adjusted the wedding arrangement of red roses and baby's breath that Dana had recreated for Betty, but I feared that there would be no bride walking down the aisle for a second round this lifetime. Love had made me such a fool. Betty wasn't coming. She had no intention of taking me back.

"How much longer do you want to wait, Reggie?" Father Erikson asked from the altar. I had almost forgotten that he was to play an integral part in my plan. Honouring my wishes for a perfect vow renewal, he came forward to replace a couple of melted candles.

"Five more minutes, please," I begged nervously. Then, he left me alone with my thoughts. It was 6:15 p.m. I was more convinced that she wasn't coming. I stood, about to enter the vestry and tell Father Erikson that it was time to call it a night. But, just at that moment, I felt a rush of cold air and then the heavy, oak church doors closed with a bang.

"Reginald?" My name echoed through the empty building. "It's me."

Almost forgetting where I was or what I was doing I had to stifle a curse because I hated being called by my formal name. Then, I realized that there was only one person who called me that. Betty! She's here! I put my hand over my heart, praying that she was here to tell me she loved me again.

Filled with renewed anticipation, I turned to face her. "You're here! I didn't think you'd come!" I exclaimed. I couldn't contain my excitement. I opened my arms wide, but that moment was short-lived. Betty hadn't returned my elation. The smile faded from my face. Despite my efforts, it was going to take more than gifts to win my wife back.

"You had some unexpected help." Betty walked slowly down the aisle towards me. "Otherwise, I wouldn't have come." She removed her coat and laid it over the pew in front of her. She sat and motioned for me to sit beside her.

"Who?" I asked. I was becoming uncomfortable in my clothes, even in my own skin.

"Sophia," Betty said flatly.

"Why would she suggest that you meet me?" I asked, dumbfounded.

"She's sick of all the gifts that keep showing up at the house. There are so many arrangements that their fragrance is overbearing," she complained timidly.

Did I just see the trace of a smile on Betty's face as she chastised me for my expressions of love? Dare I hope that my gestures got through to her after all?

"Dana did a good job, didn't she?" I said, searching for validation.

"Uh huh. It seems as if you're keeping her in business."

Did I see a twinkle in her eye when she said that? "I was just trying to win you back," I confessed.

"You never lost me, you old fool." Betty gently hit my shoulder with her hand. "And you don't need to win me back with wedding vows, either. I just want you to say nice things to me occasionally." She crossed her arms. "I want you to appreciate me more."

I winced at the pain from her words. I released a breath of pent-up air from deep within me, relieved that things might be on the mend between us, if I made more of an effort.

"Why would I waste 39 years of marriage over a petty fight?" Betty sighed and gazed at me. A kaleidoscope of memories flashed before my eyes. We've had many good years together, and some not so good ones too – but who doesn't? "You can be exasperating, but we've had a long, mostly happy life together. I'm not about to end it now."

"It's 40 years today, Mrs. Snow," I added wistfully.

"That's right. Today's Boxing Day, isn't it?" Betty dropped back into the pew, surprised at how many years we had spent as husband and wife. "Just like that, four decades together." She snapped her fingers, signalling the lightyears that had just flown by.

"You're still as beautiful as ever," I whispered to her. A twinkle gleamed in my eyes, not unlike the star on top of the Christmas tree. I moved forward and laid my forehead against her shoulder. I was tired of beating myself up for my mistakes. I was done missing her. She leaned into me, sensing my remorse, and rested her head on top of mine. We sat in silence for a moment, absorbing each other's emotions, reflecting on the time we have been wed.

Memories flashed by like faded photographs and silent films: our wedding, birthdays, and the birth of our daughter. All the moments we shared, good and bad, whizzed past. As I smiled, tears filled my eyes. Betty quickly wiped them away, knowing I wasn't one to show my emotions.

"I should have tried harder," I admitted. "You deserved more from me." I stared down at my calloused hands.

"You've been a good husband, Reggie." Betty's hand reached down. She laced her fingers between mine and gave a gentle squeeze. "But you could've listened a little better," she said firmly. I knew those words to be true.

"I should have stayed so we could've talked, instead of leaving and going to Sophia's. That wasn't fair to you." Betty scolded herself so as not to entirely blame me.

"It's been a *long* couple of months, more like an eternity," I drawled.

"I was hurt, and I wanted to teach you a lesson." Betty's chuckle was the most beautiful thing I have ever heard, even to this very day.

"Lesson learned," I said, and we both laughed.

Seizing the moment I gingerly said, "Since today is our 40th wedding anniversary, maybe we should celebrate." I held my breath waiting for Betty's reaction.

Betty lifted her hands to showcase the decorations around the church. I didn't think she had noticed, but she was here, and she was wearing that beautiful dress I sent.

"It's a shame to waste all of this," she suggested. "But Reggie, we already had a wedding." She clutched my hand. "I don't need to renew my vows with you to prove to you how much I love you."

"I know," I agreed, "except I owe you a proper honeymoon."

"A honeymoon?" she asked, bemused.

"You always dreamed about going to Hawaii." I reached into my jacket pocket and pulled out an envelope, handed it to her and watched as she opened it.

"A two week cruise to Hawaii!" She squealed with delight. "Is this really happening?"

"I've been working on changing my priorities the last couple of months, hoping to surprise you." Betty lunged at me, finally embracing me in her arms. I was wrapped in the loving arms of my wife once again. "Just don't expect any more daily gifts. I won't be able to afford the trip if I continue with these grand gestures." That, and I was sure Dana's flower fridge was damn near empty because of me.

"Aren't I worth it?" Betty jested, sinking into me.

"I was hoping this trip would shut you up," I cracked at her.

"Reggie, maybe you haven't changed a bit." She swatted at my wrist. "But don't ever change, I love you just as you are." She took a free hand and lifted it towards my face. She clutched my chin and gave my jolly, pink cheeks a shake. "I love you, you fool."

"I love you, too, Mrs. Snow." And with that, I kissed my Boxing Day Bride on the lips.

"Cheers to 40 more years," she cooed.

"If we're lucky," I smiled and leaned in to kiss my wife again. But before our lips could touch again, my lips parted, realizing I had forgotten something. I got up, scooted past my wife, and headed towards the altar.

"I almost forgot something," I said, out of breath, as I rushed back to my wife. "The kiss doesn't count unless it's under this." I dangled the fresh, green mistletoe over our heads and wiggled my eyebrows. Betty laughed again and kissed me.

We may not have renewed our vows tonight, but my faith in our love was renewed. Sharing how we'd shown up for each other meant more than recycling a wedding day we already enjoyed several decades ago.

"Okay, you old romantic. It's time to go home. I miss my Brucie."

Home, I sighed to myself.

After donning our winter apparel, we linked arms and headed into the cool night air. We returned to the life we shared and would continue to share for many more years to come.

CHAPTER 57
Wyatt

I couldn't help but feel like a man of missed opportunities.

First, I chickened out on proposing to Sabrina at the Christmas Eve Market because Tom showed up. I didn't want to upstage Dana after all she had been through, and I was genuinely happy for both of them. I couldn't help but feel a small pang of sadness to see my first love fall back into love with her first love. But people move on. I did.

Then, there was Christmas morning. Rachel had been urging me to give Sabrina grandma's wedding ring that morning. She seemed to think that opening a red velvet box would create memories to last a lifetime —a romantic story to pass on to our children one day. I panicked. What if Sabrina said 'no'? I'd be embarrassed in front of my family, and I would've risked ruining Christmas for everyone.

I watched as Sabrina rattled every box under the tree and excitedly tore into the paper, eager to see what she had been gifted. I think she was disappointed when she opened the last small box containing not *the* ring, but a gift card to a store she liked.

Christmas was as expected. Dad invited Marnie over, which is something I'm still getting used to. Now that they didn't have to keep their relationship a secret, they held hands and made plans for a romantic winter getaway. It was nice to see my dad so happy.

Later, as I helped Rachel to load her bags into the trunk of her car she looked at me and said, "So that's it? You've changed your mind *again*." My sister always cuts right to the bone about things. "You didn't ask her to marry you! What's wrong with you anyway?" she said with obvious disgust.

I was at a loss for words. I was disappointed in myself, and Rachel was twisting the knife, making me feel even worse.

"When are you going to bite the bullet and ask her?" Rachel whined. "Aren't you afraid she'll move on?"

The possibility of losing Sabrina hadn't really occurred to me. Quite possibly, Rachel could see the horror of that thought on my face and she tried to walk back her words.

"Wy, I love you." She swatted me playfully to break the tension. I couldn't resist returning the swat before backing away and then laughing at her. She hastily made a snowball and threw it at me, but I ducked and ran behind the car.

"Promise me, you'll think about it," Rachel said as she opened the driver's door and climbed in. "Sabrina is the one. Don't let her get away." I knew that she meant well, but I just wanted people to leave me alone. I didn't need the pressure, but her words resonated with me.

I watched as Rachel pulled out of the driveway. As much as I hate goodbyes, I knew I'd see my little sister again in a couple of months for Dad's birthday. I had other things to tend to, and one less distraction helped.

I wondered about the man I was destined to become. I thought about my dad and Reggie. Damn, I hope his wife comes back to him, I do. Maybe I'd see him after he comes back from Toronto and catch up with him.

***

After Rachel left, things returned to normal. Over the holidays, the shop was slow. We had a few people passing through with flat tires or chipped windshields from the transports kicking up rocks on the highway. Dad had given Fletcher and some of the other guys the week off, so it was just him and me in the shop. I wished I had some extra time off, too, with Sabrina, but she had been keeping busy down at the curling rink. That woman could never sit still for long. Sometimes I thought she was avoiding me because I still couldn't commit to forever with her, and other times I figured she was just doing her own thing; it was hard to say.

On New Year's Eve we planned to close the shop early. Dad and Marnie were anxious to head out to Niagara Falls for a concert, so I offered to stay late and finish the repair job that we had been working on. Besides, Sabrina and I had our own plans; we were going to order takeout and watch a movie to ring in the New Year.

Dad came over and patted me on the back as I wiped motor oil off my hands. They were blackened from the automotive fluids I was working with. "You and Sabrina have a nice night. We'll see you when we get back."

As he headed out the shop door, I called out to him, "Give Marnie my best for the New Year." I wanted Dad to know that I was accepting of their relationship, even if I hadn't quite vocalized that yet.

"Thanks, son. I will." And with that, he was off.

I was in the shop alone with my thoughts. I had been mulling over in my head Rachel's warning that Sabrina might move on without me. I knew what I wanted. I had been putting off the inevitable for too damn long. Without any hesitation, I opened the drawer of my workstation, reached in and took out the ring box. I put it in my pocket, took a deep breath, and headed home.

***

On the way, I stopped to pick up a bottle of the sparkling wine Sabrina liked. She giggled like a kid whenever she drank it because the bubbles tickled her nose. I loved to make her laugh. It was one of my favourite things about her.

It was a little later than I had intended to get home, but there was still time for some snuggling and kissing before the countdown. The house, however, was in complete darkness, and when I entered, the quiet enveloped me. I was grateful that all my family was away, but where was Sabrina? I called out her name, but there was no answer at first.

"In here!" Her faint voice called out; I couldn't quite tell which room she was in. At least she was home. That was a relief, but what was she up to?

When I rounded the corner, a trail of red rose petals and a line of pillar candles beckoned me to follow their path. "What's going on?" I called out.

"You'll see," Sabrina called out sweetly.

My heart was racing. My expectations were soaring. As I entered the living room I beheld my beautiful girlfriend in a flowing white dress standing in front of a glowing fireplace.

"Sabrina," I gasped, "what is this?" I moved forward, reaching for her hand. Her fingers laced between mine, and she gave me a gentle squeeze. Her radiant smile illuminated the room.

"I think you know what this is," she winked at me.

How could I not? I replied, "I know it's taken me a long time to do this. I wanted to ask you, but I doubted myself." She placed her fingers to my lips, silencing me.

"It isn't your responsibility to propose marriage." She pulled at the hem of her dress, letting the material billow over the hardwood floor. "I'm a modern woman after all," she chided.

She sure was a modern woman. She didn't need me in her life; she could look after herself. The difference was that she wanted me in her life, which was way sexier. "I know, but it's been your dream for me to ask you to marry me." My palms were sweaty.

"No, Wyatt, it's our dream to end up together. How it happens doesn't matter, so long as it happens." Damn, I love this woman. "So, that's what we are talking about tonight: our forever." She stood on her tippy toes so that her soft lips could meet mine. That kiss, man. I longed for those kisses. The touch of her lips warmed my weary heart.

"Wyatt, I still remember the first time I saw you. That first lunch with you and Dana was one of the best days of my life." Her pearly white teeth flashed me the biggest grin. "There was something about the way you smiled at me that lit up my whole world. You know, I used to write your name on all my schoolbooks, hoping that one day you'd ask me to be your girlfriend." She snuffled, tears forming in the corner of her eyes.

"Sab," I took a rough finger and gently wiped them away.

"You've brought so much light into my life," she snuffled again. I leaned over and handed her a tissue. "I know that you haven't had it easy, but we are good for each other. With you, everything feels possible."

As if trying to calm herself, she smoothed down her dress and went on, "I don't expect much. I don't need a ring, a fancy wedding or even a marriage certificate. All I need is you and your love." Her voice quivered. I wasn't sure what was about to come next. "Wyatt Mason Greene, will you promise to be my boyfriend and *not* marry me?" We both laughed.

This was not how I planned the proposal. I was going to get down on one knee, tell her how much I loved her, show her the ring, and ask her to be my wife. Then, she would say 'yes', throw her arms around me and we would kiss.

When I hesitated, lost for words because my plan had flown out the window, she started to back away. Tears started to stream down her face, leaving a thin river of mascara trickling down her cheeks.

"Sabrina, wait. It's not like that."

"Then what is it? Don't you love me?" She looked away, likely afraid of my answer.

I gasped. "Of course I love you, that's not what this is about."

"Then what is it about?" She asked. "Have I given you reason to doubt my love for you?"

"Never, I…" I stuttered.

"I'm not your mom!" She wailed.

Those words knocked the wind out of me. She understandably had misconstrued my reason for being hesitant when she proposed to me.

"I didn't say I didn't want to marry you, Sab," I said. "It's just that I had this proposal thing all worked out in my head. I wasn't expecting you to take the initiative."

She shook her head at me, not sure what to think. All I could do was to show her what I truly wanted. With one swift motion, I bent a knee. I reached into my breast pocket, pulled out the small box, and opened the lid. Inside, a small family heirloom sparkled in the light of the fireplace.

Sabrina gasped. "Is that what I think it is?" She clasped a hand over her mouth in shock.

"It's Grandma Greene's wedding ring. Dad saved it for me. He wanted me to give it to the woman I wanted to marry, and that's you." My eyes twinkled as I found hers again.

"Wyatt, are you sure?" The hurricane of emotions calmed and turned back to love.

"As sure as a heart attack." We both laughed.

"You know, you'd be stuck with me forever," she warned.

"Yeah, I'm good with that."

I slipped the ring on Sabrina's finger, promising her a love to last forever – and I meant it.

In my heart of hearts, I've always known she was the one. I had a feeling, way back when, that the girl in the cafeteria with the green and blue braces on her teeth would one day be my bride. And now, Sabrina and I could focus on our own happily ever after.

EPILOGUE

And so, our holiday tales of love, laughter, and the occasional festive fiasco come to a close.

Our three merry misfits, Dana, Reggie, and Wyatt, each searched their hearts and somehow, against all odds, stumbled into the love they'd been searching for... or, in some cases, avoiding.

Maybe it was the twinkling Christmas lights, the sugar overload from one too many of Marnie's brownies, or the fact that mistletoe seemed to be strewn all over Mercer, thanks to Dana. Whatever the reason, the spell of love was cast.

Dana discovered that love isn't defined by her mistakes, and that it's okay to be imperfect. In the end, she unexpectedly rekindled her romance with her first love, Tom. He eventually decided to make the move back to Mercer, working remotely. They enjoy working in the shop together, snuggling with Ruby and double dating with Wyatt and Sabrina.

For Reggie, he found that sometimes, second chances are sweeter than the first ones. Love can be messy, but it's worth it. Reggie and Betty enjoyed a Hawaiian holiday. They've planned a road trip to visit Maggie in the city when the car is finally completed. As for Bruce, he'll enjoy laying in the sunbeams when his pet parents are on vacation.

And Wyatt? Well, he proved that love can be as simple as looking up from the past long enough to see the future waiting with open arms, and even a kiss. Wyatt and Sabrina are enjoying a long engagement. Maybe the wedding bells will soon ring for them, and if not, maybe they can enjoy Lou and Marnie's wedding- if they beat them to the altar. Rachel is banking on being a bridesmaid for both weddings.

In these final words, let's raise a cup of hot chocolate and make a toast: cheers to listening to your heart, risking it all, and having no regrets—because, at the end of the day, the holidays remind us that love is the best gift of all.

THANK YOU

To my family and friends: Thank you for encouraging me to write- I'm having a blast. I value your love and support.

To the readers: Thank you for taking the time to read my creative works. I hope you will consider staying along on this wild ride.

Ashley XO

About the Author

Ashley Percival is an indie author from Ontario, Canada. This is her first holiday romance novel. Ashley's other novels include:

Miss Adventures: Abroad from Bangkok to Bali, a romantic comedy which is loosely on her travels abroad. It is the first novel in the *Miss Adventures* series.

Also, *Your Lonesome Loving Harold*. This is a collection of love letters Ashley's grandfather wrote her grandmother in 1936. Ashley collaborated on this novella with her father, Gary, who is a retired high-school English teacher.

KEEP IN TOUCH

Dear Reader,
Thank you for your love and support! If you're interested in joining my Advance Reader Copy (ARC) team, please email me below. You'll receive a PDF copy of my upcoming work and book cover image to share on your socials. And, if you're excited about the book, a review on the various book platforms is always appreciated.

Much love and gratitude,
Ashley XO

Email: misadventures.media.canada@gmail.com
Socials: https://linktr.ee/misadventuresmedia

Manufactured by Amazon.ca
Bolton, ON